Serpent & Spice

Serpent & Spice

Book 1
A Serpent & Spice Adventure

SYLVIE D. HARLOWE

For Emma.
You inspire me every day.
Keep dreaming.

CONTENTS

CHAPTER 1
The Weight of Marble

Rome, 298 B.C.

The atrium air always felt the same: cool, dry, and smelling faintly of beeswax polish and the dust of generations. Lyrra traced the intricate pattern of a mosaic on the floor with the toe of her sandal, slow and exact, her path deliberately finding the one tessera set amiss—a splash of carnelian red in a sea of cool blue and white. The lifeless stone pressed back. It always did.

Lyrra Aemilia Secunda.

Secunda.

Second daughter. Second attempt. "Second helpings," if her father had ever cracked a joke about her at the dinner table. But he saved his meals for his "business partners." He'd said it once, offhand, when she was twelve. She still skipped meals sometimes without realizing.

Her older sister, Prima, had been married off at fifteen to a grain baron in Syracuse. Lyrra had seen her only once since—seated in an open carriage, veiled but visible. A delicate weave of gold filigree dotted with lapis lazuli lay across her collarbones, like a constellation of cold stars trapped in a golden web. She wore a smile. Hollow. Tight.

Until she saw Lyrra.

Then, just for a second, the real smile broke through. *That wasn't joy in her smile. It was recognition. From one prisoner to another prisoner.*

In House Aemilius, daughters weren't named so much as catalogued. Lyrra was next. Eighteen years old—three years past her sister's age and, by her father's calculation, already a depreciating asset. To her father, daughters were units of strategic leverage: dressed, braided, and delivered.

Lucius Aemilius Gallus, her father—his voice, a deep, resonant baritone that had dictated the rhythm of life—echoed from the study. Each word was measured, precise. Sharp little chips. How a sculptor works marble.

Wait. Did he just say my name?

The rough grain of the study's locked side door was a sudden, cool shock against her cheek. She hadn't meant to move. But there she was, pressed against the wood.

"...an alliance of considerable strategic value. Gisco's family controls the grain shipments from North Africa. Securing this union will guarantee our access for the next decade. Her passage to Carthage is already booked; she departs in two days."

Two days. The mosaic floor dropped out from under her. Two days, and she would be gone. Two days, and she would cease to be Lyrra. Only a *thing* of *value.*

Lyrra pressed her ear closer to the door, her lips thinning into a line. *Asset. Alliance.* The words weren't about people; they were about ledgers, about trade routes, about the careful, calculated accumulation of power. Her life was just another number noted in the margins of her father's account book. She wasn't even an entry. She was a *placeholder* for one.

A soft rustle of fabric announced her mother's entrance. Domitia's posture was flawless. She moved like she was always on display, every fold of her stola arranged just so, every pin in her hair catching the light. A practiced grace, each gesture careful, every smile perfect.

"Lyrra, darling," she said, smooth as always. "Your father wishes you to join him. Senator Varro is here. He has news of the latest shipment from Hispania."

Lyrra nodded, her throat tight. She smoothed her tunic, pale and plain beside Domitia's deep imperial purple.

She didn't shine. *That was the point.*

The sight of her mother's purple silk billowing as she walked made her own white linen tunic feel like a burlap sackcloth against her skin. *Just once, Mother. See me. Not as some doll. Not 'Secunda.' Me.*

As she followed her mother towards the study's main door, she passed the great fresco that dominated the hall wall. It depicted a scene of Roman triumph—soldiers marching, banners flying, a defeated barbarian king kneeling. Lyrra paused, her gaze caught on the stoic faces of the Roman legionaries—blank and polished like their helmets. Loyal. Unyielding. Devoid of emotion. Instruments of control.

A low "Ugh" from deep in her gut escaped her. Her mother didn't notice. *She never did.*

Lyrra suddenly wanted a honey-cake from the kitchens. They were off limits. Forbidden.

Gods, I could just break something. A heat flared low in her chest. *A vase. A bowl. To feel something—anything!*

The urge to snatch a vase from its pedestal and hurl it against the wall was so strong that her muscles trembled with the effort of restraint. *A crack. A shatter. Any sound but his voice.*

But the echo of her father's voice, the gleam of her mother's purple, the painted soldiers' unblinking judgment—they all pressed down on her, stripping her of that desire. Numb.

She drew a sharp breath. The air in her lungs was thin. Already depleted.

Her thoughts of cake and chaos vanished. But the heat and pressure stayed, collapsing inward into a single point of purpose in her chest. Her breath evened out. The air didn't feel so thin anymore.

She turned and ran with one thought in her mind: *I know where they keep the servants' tunics.*

CHAPTER 2
An Instrument of Rebellion

The rough wool of the servant's tunic scratched at her skin, a welcome, grounding irritation. Her father's words—*asset, alliance, guarantee*—kept scratching at the inside of her mind. But her body… that was the one territory her father's ledgers and Gisco's pronouncements couldn't fully claim. And tonight, she would be its sole sovereign.

Her hands shook as she pulled the dark hood over her patrician hair, tucking away the last traces of Lyrra, daughter of Lucius Aemilius Gallus. Each fold of the coarse fabric was a small act of erasure. In the silent, polished corridors of her home, she was an asset. Out in the streets, she would be no one. A shaky gasp escaped her mouth. *Finally, I'm out. I'm free.*

Slipping through a side gate beside manicured gardens, the city's chaos slammed into her. The thick air was a foul stew of roasting meat, cheap wine, and the unwashed sweat of a thousand bodies. She faltered, the chaos overwhelming. Then she saw her sister's face in her mind—that perfected smile. She saw herself wearing the same smile, a pretty, silent object on the arm of a man who would admire her like a trophy won. The image settled like a sickness deep in her stomach. *I will not wear that smile.*

The taberna was a roar of slurred voices and clattering dice, the air thick with spilled wine and hot bodies. Lyrra clutched the few quadrans she'd taken in her sweaty palm, her heart hammering against her ribs. Her gaze swept the room, a desperate search for her would-be first partner. She saw only a blur of leering faces. Nameless. Panic threatened to send her fleeing back to her cage. *Is there anyone suitable? Is this it?*

Then she saw him.

He wasn't the most handsome man in the room, nor the youngest. But his shoulders were broad under worn leather, his hands callused around a clay cup. He laughed, a loud, unthinking sound that held no cunning. Not a politician. Not a nobleman. He was a simple, physical force. *An easy choice.*

Perfect.

The instrument of her rebellion.

When she finally approached, his wine-bleary gaze took her in with a slow, deliberate survey. "Lost, little dove?"

"Perhaps I wish to be," she managed.

It was enough. He shot her a well-rehearsed grin, but his gaze remained flat and assessing. "Follow me," he said, already turning toward the back. "I know a quieter place."

The alley was cold, the tavern noise a muffled pulse. He pressed her backward against a stone wall—damp, rough, smelling of refuse. His mouth came down on hers. Hungry. Demanding. Heat and wine, all at once. For a dizzying second, she was just a girl, out of her depth. Then, the fire in her chest answered back. *This is mine. All mine.*

She kissed him back, a clumsy but fierce collision. *I am the one who chooses. Here, I have the power.* A territory she had never dared to explore, now suddenly within her grasp.

He broke the kiss, breathing hard. "Gods, you are a flame," he growled, but his eyes held a new, calculating light. His touch shifted. The hand that had guided her was now clenched, his fingers digging into the soft flesh of her arm.

A claim.

The thought was cold water down her back. Every muscle went rigid. *This is not what I wanted.*

He saw her stiffen and his face hardened, something cold in his eyes. "Don't play coy now," he snarled, misreading her fear as a game. He shoved her back, the impact knocking the air from her lungs. His rough grip on her arms was bruising. The heat she'd felt moments before turned to ice.

"Stop," she whispered, her voice a pathetic squeak.

He laughed, a low, ugly sound. "*You* came with me, little dove." He pinned her wrists with one hand and fumbled with her tunic with the other.

The alley walls seemed to rush inward, the sounds of the tavern dissolving into a distant, meaningless hum.

What's happening to me? What will *happen to me?*

The cold stone at her back. The calculating light in his eyes. The hands of a stranger.

Mistake. Wrong. Get out.

A sharp scrape of a sandal on stone from the alley's mouth. A woman's annoyed voice. "There you are, you drunken lout, I knew I'd find you—" The voice cut off, then erupted in fury. "Get your filthy hands off my husband, you gutter-rat!"

A small, furious woman with eyes like black coals stood there, her gaze flicking to Lyrra with immediate, venomous contempt. The legionary froze, stumbling back. "Fulvia! It's not what you think. This girl, she's a whore—"

Lyrra didn't wait. The woman's attack, the names lobbed at her, were burnt into her like brands. *Gutter-rat? Whore? Is that what this makes me? Is that all I can be?*

She fled, pushing past the furious wife and running blindly into the dark streets. All she could hear was the word *whore* echoing in her ears. Her only thought was to outrun the eyes that she could still feel burning into her back.

Back in the cold silence of her room, she stared at her reflection. A stranger looked back, her face pale, her eyes hollow. She scrubbed at her mouth, but it wasn't the taste of wine she was trying to erase. It was the sour tang of her own foolishness.

CHAPTER 3
The Salt-Stained Cage

The world had muted. The sharp scent of beeswax polish in the atrium was a memory. The cold of the marble floor no longer registered through the thin leather of her sandals. She stood, arms limp at her sides, while her mother fussed with the folds of a new stola, her touch no more meaningful than a breeze.

As her departure drew near, she allowed her mother to oversee the packing of her dowry chests, her sullen silence mistaken for maidenly modesty. When her mother held up the silver hand mirror, Lyrra's gaze slid past her own reflection, fixing on the wall behind her. She remembered its intricate carvings, her own laughing face once reflected there. *How naive.* Now, the thought of looking into it sparked no warmth. *You won't know the person you see.*

Departing from the port of Ostia was a brisk, business-like affair. Her father stood before her on the bustling quay, his face as impassive. He placed a heavy pendant in her palm—a glass cameo rimmed with gold. It was intricately carved with the bust of Juno, goddess of marriage and duty. His touch was as lifeless as the pendant itself.

"This was your mother's," he said, his tone that of a magistrate signing a transfer of property. "Do not disgrace it. Do not disgrace me."

It's too late for that, the thought came, sharp as a shard of glass. *I am already a disgrace. A disgrace of my own making. But at least that is mine.*

There was no embrace. No warmth in his eyes. He turned and walked away, his duty done.

A guard gestured toward the gangplank. Lyrra's feet felt like lead as she walked the narrow plank, the sounds of the port fading. She did not look back. Not until the ship lurched, pulling away from the dock, did she finally turn.

Lyrra watched the shoreline of Italia dissolve into a hazy, indifferent line. She should feel something. Grief, fear, anger. Nothing. That girl who had run into that alley was gone, leaving this husk in her place.

○　○　○　○　○

The ship had been a floating cell for a day or two. But now, the ceaseless groaning of the hull had finally settled into a low, resentful creak against the dock. Through the small, salt-crusted porthole of her cabin, she could see the lights of a city climbing a dark hill, a scattered constellation of man-made stars.

Syracuse. Prima's city.

Lyrra lay on her narrow cot, listening. The distant sounds were different from the open sea. These were the sounds of land, of life: shouted orders in a dialect of Greek she barely understood, the rumble of carts on stone, and the raucous, booming laughter of men spilling from waterfront taverns.

That sound—that deep laughter—was a hook. It snagged on a memory and pulled, dragging her from the relative safety of her cabin back to the alley outside the taberna in Rome.

The memory suddenly slammed into her body. The wood beneath her back felt as cold and damp as the alley wall. The air, thick with salt, now sour with the scent of his wine-soaked breath.

The weight of him, a crushing, indifferent force, and the low, ugly sound of his laugh just before his wife's furious shout had saved her.

Lyrra's eyes flew open, her heart a frantic drumming staccato. The memory wasn't just in her head. It was in the room with her. The darkness was heavy. Pressing. The air was suddenly impossible to breathe.

The space was a coffin. She knew if she stretched out her legs, her toes would brush the far wall. The low ceiling seemed to descend, its weight settling on her chest, pinning her down.

Pinned. Can't move.

She couldn't breathe. Helpless again by the very architecture of her own confinement. A scream built in her throat, but she swallowed it. Her own mind was shouting the words, a frantic command to her own frozen limbs.

Get out. Get out. GET OUT.

She managed to scramble from the cot, her bare feet hitting the cold floor. Her hands shook as she fumbled for the door's latch, her fingers slick with a sweat that had nothing to do with heat. Her breath came in ragged, useless gasps. The door gave way. She didn't hesitate. She fled, stumbling out of the cabin and into the narrow companionway. She needed air. She needed the sky.

The night air on the main deck hit her like a physical blow. Cold. Salty. Real. She gulped it down in ragged, desperate breaths, her lungs burning with the relief of it. The panic began to recede, leaving her shaking and hollowed out.

She moved from the open, a shadow seeking deeper shadows. She found a spot deep in the darkness behind a stack of canvas-covered crates, a place where no one would look, where no one would see. She sank to the deck, wrapping her arms around her knees, making herself small. Unseen. Safe.

She listened to her own ragged breathing, a stark contrast to the distant chaos of the port. Her heart slowed. She was back to the present.

Then, a new sound cut through the night.

It wasn't the creak of the ship's hull or the slap of water against wood. This was closer. A soft, rhythmic thud. *Thud. Thud.* The sound of a body hitting wood. Then a man's low, guttural grunt.

Her first instinct was to make herself smaller, a reflexive flinch away from the sound of a man's exertion.

But then another sound joined it. A woman's breathy sigh, a soft moan that held no trace of pain. It was a sound of… pleasure.

The need to stay hidden warred with a new, sharp impulse. This was a different kind of sound than the one from her memory. This was not the sound of a struggle.

She had to see. She had to *know*.

She rose from her crouch, her movements slow and deliberate. She kept to the deepest parts of the shadows, her bare feet silent on the worn wood of the deck. The sounds grew louder, more distinct now. The steady, driving rhythm of the creaking wood. The man's harsh, ragged breathing. The woman's moans were no longer soft sighs. They were low, open-throated sounds. Undeniably, shockingly, sounds of pleasure.

She reached the edge of the stacked crates and peered through a narrow gap, her heart beating heavy in her ears.

The swinging light of a single lantern cut the scene out of the darkness. She saw him first: a sailor, broad and bearded, a wall of muscle and sweat. His rough trousers bunched around his knees, his muscles strained with every animalistic push. Her eyes drifted down to the thick, slick length of him as he drove into her. *A weapon*, she thought. *A battering ram.*

He had a woman bent over a large crate, her dress hiked to her waist.

Her breasts. Her breasts are just... out. They hung over the top of the bunched fabric, heavy and pale, swinging free with every rocking motion.

A Roman woman would die of shame.

Her dress was a ruin, her hair a mess of black curls, plastered to her cheek with sweat. She reached up with one hand, Lyrra expecting her to push him away, to fight.

But she didn't.

She just swiped the damp curls from her eyes. A practical gesture. *So she can see better? No*, Lyrra thought, *so she can* feel *better.*

Lyrra's Roman brain screamed. *Vulgar. Base.*

But her eyes told a different story. She could not look away.

The sailor's hands were on the woman's hips—big, callused hands that weren't pinning or gripping. They were guiding, his thumbs rubbing slow circles on the swell of her ass. Her hips rolled back to meet his every thrust, a slow, deliberate grind.

Then, the woman threw her head back, her face catching the full lantern light. Her eyes were squeezed shut, her lips parted. And she was smiling. A feral grin of unthinking pleasure.

Lyrra's breath caught. Her entire education crumbled to dust.

She let out a sharp, audible gasp in the dark. A voice in her head—her mother's... no, all the matrons of Rome—screamed. *Vulgar. Whore.*

Her body refused to listen. It only cared about the woman's smile. That feral grin. Her body asked a question she couldn't un-ask.

Can I feel that? That grin? That release?

Is that... possible for me?

The sounds from the couple continued—the soft, wet slap of their bodies, the woman's moans becoming sharper, more urgent. A rhythm. A permission.

Her hand moved, a slow, unstoppable journey beneath the hem of her tunic. The cool night air a shock against her warm skin. Her fingers brushed against the soft curls between her legs as she slid them into the thin linen of her undergarment. She pressed, a broad, firm pressure of her fingertips against the mound of her sex. She was looking for the source. The root of that power.

She felt it—her fingers met a slick heat that was her own. A secret her body had kept from her.

Gods.

She held the pressure, adding a desperate side-to-side motion. And in that moment, a spark ignited deep inside her. Not pain, not shame, but something else entirely.

A final, sharp cry from the woman, a guttural groan from the man, and then... silence.

The sudden quiet pulled Lyrra from the haze of her own discovery back to the world outside her skin. The sway of the ship. The black deck. Her own body still trembling. The sailor pulled away, his movements slower now. He gave the woman's hip a rough but not unkind pat and began pulling his trousers up. He leaned in close, his voice a low rumble she couldn't make out.

The woman didn't reply with words. She just let out a small, weary laugh and gave his arm a light, dismissive shove.

He held out his hand, the glint of a few coins in his open palm. She didn't snatch them. She simply held out her own, and he pressed them into her palm, his callused fingers brushing against hers for a moment longer than necessary.

They separated without another look, two people moving on with their night. Lyrra was left alone in the shadows, her hand still pressed against herself, her body shaking. She slowly straightened up, her legs unsteady. The cold was still there—the ship, the sea, the man in Carthage waiting to claim her. That hadn't changed.

But it was no longer absolute.

She waited for it. The disgust. The Roman shame.

It didn't come.

It is possible.

I am not broken.

o   o   o   o   o

The morning after, Lyrra woke to the familiar creak of the hull, the memory of the cabin's crushing darkness now pushed to the edge of her thoughts. She waited for the panic to return.

It didn't.

Instead, another image rose in her mind, unbidden: the woman the night before, head thrown back, breasts out, a feral grin of pleasure on her face. *This was real.*

She held onto that image, that feeling.

The memory of the alley was a story of what could be done *to* her. The memory of the woman was a story of what could be done *for* her.

She had to remind herself: *I survived the alley. I survived the screaming chorus of Roman matrons in my mind. I survived my own shame.*

All that was left was a quiet truth.

After that, the endless grey of the sea felt… simple. Manageable. *I will survive this too.*

The frequent drone of sailors' voices outside her cabin was a meaningless tide, washing against the shores of her misery. Most of it dissolved into noise, their voices rough from sun and salt. Until a name, spoken with a raspy chuckle, snagged on the edge of her awareness: "Hanno."

"Aye, Hanno," said the second voice. "They say he charmed a Nubian princess right out from under her father's nose for a sack of royal myrrh—the kind only queens can afford."

"I heard he outwitted a Cyclops for a load of Tyrian purple," the first sailor shot back, the lie so grand it was almost a form of respect. "Point is, the man's a legend in the Carthage market. Sells the scent of paradise but walks through hell to get it. Patrician ladies and temple prostitutes, they all pay his price."

"He's a merchant, not a god," the second grumbled, though there was envy in his tone. "A silver-tongued serpent, more like. Best keep your wife and your coin purse away from him."

Lyrra leaned her head against the rough wood of the door. Hanno. The name was foreign, exotic. *A silver-tongued serpent.* The men she knew were marble statues like her father, or brutes like the legionary. They took, they commanded, they owned. But the sailors spoke of this Hanno as something else—a charmer, a trickster, a rogue. *What kind of man goes through hell for a scent?*

The question was a spark of light in the grey emptiness of her thoughts. The first thing that wasn't a memory or a fear. It was everything her world wasn't. Dangerous. Free.

It was on one such morning, indistinguishable from the last, that the world shifted. The perpetual damp chill was replaced by a caress of warmth. And the smell. It was not the familiar Italian scent of pine and cypress. This was something else entirely—warm and dusty. Baked earth, flowers, and something sharp and sweet.

Drawn by an impulse she didn't understand, Lyrra climbed the ladder to the main deck. The sun was brighter here, the sky a more brilliant blue. And there, on the horizon, was a long, pale smudge of land.

Africa.

The sailors bustled around her, preparing for landfall, but no one paid her any mind. She was just a piece of cargo, soon to be delivered. She closed her hand around the pendant at her neck. The Roman gold felt heavy and cold. An anchor to a life already deceased. Her eyes remained fixed on the growing shoreline. A land of spice. And serpents.

I am still here. This thought held no comfort, no joy. It was a simple, hard fact, like the salt on her lips.

And I will be here tomorrow.

CHAPTER 4
The Gilded Cage

The moment the ship touched the quay in Carthage, her world exploded. Noise, color, smell. Rome was quiet dust and marble order. This... this was chaos. A man shouted about dates, his voice competing with the whine of a stringed instrument. The air was thick—roasting lamb, heady perfume, and an unfamiliar spice that made Lyrra's throat burn.

Lyrra's hand tightened on the ship's railing, her knuckles white, her focus narrowing to the feel of the rough, salt-crusted wood beneath her fingers. Real. Solid. There. She stared at it, a tiny island of certainty in an overwhelming sea. Crowds pressed against the dock, held back by burly men in purple livery. They were staring. Pointing. *Wait.* A horrifying realization seeped through her numbness: they weren't just watching the ship. They were watching *her*. An unveiling.

A woman who could only be Gisco's mother moved through the crowd, which parted for her as if by divine command—or for the mother of the man who controlled their grain shipments. She was tall, dressed in shimmering sea-green silk. She stopped before Lyrra, her dark eyes taking a quick inventory. Lyrra felt a familiar coldness, a prickle on her arms, and forced herself not to flinch.

"I am Sybil," she said. Her voice was smooth, polished, and utterly devoid of warmth. "Welcome to Carthage, Lady Lyrra. Gisco is occupied with matters of state. He is eager to make your acquaintance this evening."

Lyrra managed a weak, "Thank you." Automatic. Hollow. Her Roman training kicking in.

Sybil's gaze flickered to a young woman standing just behind her. "This is Asha. She will attend to your needs."

The girl, Asha, gave Lyrra a rapid, head-to-toe scan. Quick frown. Her lips pursed. "Gods, that wool looks scratchy," she said, her voice a low murmur meant for herself, but loud enough to cut through Lyrra's mental fog. "Very... uh, durable."

For the first time since leaving Rome, a genuine, unbidden thought formed in Lyrra's mind: *No one in my father's house would ever dare say such a thing.* The thought was so unexpected it was like a small stone dropped in a pool of still water.

Asha was perhaps a year or two older than Lyrra, with sharp, clever eyes and a mouth that looked like it was permanently wrestling a smile. She stepped forward and took Lyrra's small travel satchel. "Come, my lady. Let's get you out of the sun before you melt."

Asha's firm grip on her elbow grounded her, steering her through the throng of onlookers toward an enclosed carriage. Inside the curtained box, Lyrra stared at the intricate woven screen. She traced the zagging patterns with her eyes as the city blurred past. Asha's voice cut through the haze, a running commentary, all cynical.

"That's the Temple of Eshmun. Very dramatic, but the priests are all thieves," she said, waving a dismissive hand. "Oh, and there's the estate of the Hasherbalids. Old money. So old it's crumbling."

Lyrra's Roman sensibilities made a faint protest. "Should you be saying such things?"

Asha just shrugged. "Everyone knows it. It's only a problem if you say it where they can hear you."

Gisco's villa was not on a hill, but nestled in the very heart of the Byrsa, the citadel of power. Floors of polished obsidian reflected the light from artfully placed skylights. It was stunning with the chilling stillness of a tomb.

Her chambers were breathtaking. A mosaic of a sprawling octopus covered one entire wall, its tentacles curling with unsettling realism. Her gaze fixed on a single, perfectly rendered suction cup near the corner, a small, circular world of detail that kept the whole, terrifying image at bay.

"The bath is through there," Asha said, setting down the satchel. "Scented oils are on the shelf." She paused, her sharp eyes taking in Lyrra's rigid posture and vacant stare. "Gods, you look like you've seen a ghost. Or are one. Maybe both. I'll have some fruit sent up. Try to eat it."

Asha left, and Lyrra was alone. She walked onto the balcony, a micro-choice to assess the boundaries of her new prison. Her gaze drifted past the tinkling fountains, past the exotic blossoms, and fixed on the high walls that surrounded the garden. She reached out and touched the cool marble of the balustrade. It felt just like the marble in her father's atrium: beautiful, expensive, and utterly impassable. *Great. Just perfect.* Her fingers went to the cameo pendant at her neck, its weight a constant, solid pressure.

CHAPTER 5
The Collector

Lyrra stood like a statue while Asha fussed with the drape of a sheer, indigo blue shawl over her shoulders. The clothes were a second skin she hadn't asked for, clinging and whispering with every breath. To cope, Lyrra focused on a single thread in the fabric, tracing its path with her eyes, keeping everything else blurred and distant. *Safe.*

"Hold still," Asha commanded, tugging the fabric. Her voice was a sharp, welcome anchor in the fog. "This color makes your eyes look like the sea before a storm. Gisco likes storms. He thinks they're 'dramatic'." She said the word with a subtle roll of her eyes. "Just try not to mention his cousin's new villa in Hispania. He's terribly jealous of the mosaics."

Lyrra's head was spinning. In Rome, the rules were simple: honor the gods, your family, and the state. Here, the rules were a maze of gossip, envy, and interior design. Exhausting.

A servant in purple livery appeared at the doorway and struck a small gong. "The master Gisco."

Gisco walked in as if addressing the senate. His smile was as bright and cold as a freshly minted denarius. He was, she noted with a sinking heart, flawlessly handsome. *Perfect dark hair. Sharp jaw. Expensive tunic.* He was a perfect stranger.

"Lady Lyrra," he said, his voice a smooth, calculated balm. "Welcome. I trust my mother and the staff have made you feel at home."

"Your hospitality has been generous," Lyrra replied, her voice stiff with Roman formality, a script learned by rote.

He tilted his head, a gesture of thoughtful listening she felt certain he had practiced in a mirror. "Excellent. Your journey was pleasant, I trust? The seas can be so unpredictable."

"The seas were as the gods willed them."

His smile didn't falter, but his eyes swept over her, from the pearls Asha had woven into her hair down to the delicate, dyed leather sandals on her feet. Not desire. Assessment.

"The artisans of Carthage are skilled, but Roman beauty has a certain… solidity. A noble gravity," he announced. "You will be a welcome addition to our city."

He took a step closer, extending his hand. Lyrra's breath caught. *The collector's hand.* Her shoulders tensed, a barely perceptible tightening as she fought the urge to flinch. She forced her own hand to move, to place it in his.

His fingers were cool and dry, the grip firm but brief. She had braced for something gross. Sweaty palms, maybe. But it was not moist. There was no warmth, only a smooth, weightless contact. He released her hand, the transaction complete.

He released her hand. "I have matters of the council to attend to, but we will speak more at the evening meal. We are having a small gathering tonight. A few dozen of my closest associates. I am eager to present you."

And with another perfect, vacant smile, he turned and was gone.

The scent of his citrus cologne lingered. It was clean and sharp, a scent designed to announce its own cost and nothing more. Lyrra stood frozen, the silk on her arms feeling impossibly heavy. Silent. Thick. Suffocating.

Then, from beside her, Asha let out a quiet sigh.

"Well," she said, her voice dry as dust. "He's got all his teeth. It's a start."

A small, choked sound escaped Lyrra's lips. It was a laugh. A broken, horrified, but genuine laugh. The first real sound she'd made since leaving Rome. It was the sound of a crack appearing in the ice.

CHAPTER 6
Spice and Secrets

The gathering was not small. The hall was a crush of bodies, a blur of shimmering silk and suffocating perfume. Lyrra felt like a prize cow at market, prodded and appraised. Gisco kept her arm tucked firmly in his, guiding her from one cluster of perfumed guests to another. The performance was flawless. He would smile, introduce her, and accept their effusive praise.

"A true daughter of Mars!" a fat senator declared, looking her up and down. "Look at that profile! Pure patrician blood. Gisco, you've outdone yourself."

"She is a credit to her city, and soon to ours," Gisco would reply smoothly, his fingers giving her arm a proprietary squeeze that felt less like affection and more like a brand.

On and on it went. A woman with enough gold in her hair to ransom a king complimented Lyrra's "quaint simplicity." A man whose tunic was so fine it was nearly transparent asked if it was true that Romans only bathed once a week. They smiled at her, but their eyes were sharp, calculating. They weren't meeting *her*. They were sizing up Gisco.

The air grew thick. Jasmine incense. Sweaty bodies. Heat. Too much. Then some grinning politician patted her arm. "Fine piece of Roman marble," he said. "Solid and dependable."

Rage, cold and sharp, cut through the jasmine haze and her numbness.

"I require a moment," she murmured to Gisco, her voice tight. "The heat…"

Before he could protest, she slipped away, moving through the throng like a swimmer fighting her way to the surface. She found a set of glass doors and pushed through them, stumbling onto a dark, quiet terrace.

The cool night air was a balm. She leaned against the marble balustrade, taking deep, shuddering breaths and watching the distant lights of the lower city glitter.

"Hiding from the peacocks?"

A voice from the shadows made her jump. Low, amused. A man stepped forward—not dressed like the others. No expensive silks. He wore a simple, dark linen tunic of high quality but no ornament. The starlight caught the glint of a scar through his eyebrow.

"Or just admiring their plumage from a safe distance?" he added, a smile playing on his lips.

A genuine retort, something sharp and Roman, rose to her lips, but died there. *Peacocks.* The word was so perfect, so dismissive. "Something like that," she managed, a tiny, unexpected smile tugging at her own mouth.

He took a sip from a plain clay cup he held. "They can be a bit much. All that preening requires a tremendous amount of energy." He looked her over, his gaze direct but not invasive. "You don't look like one of them."

"I am not," she said, more fiercely than she intended.

He smiled again, a real smile that reached his eyes. He held out the cup. "You look like you could use this more than I could."

She hesitated for only a second before taking it. The clay was cool against her fingers. She lifted it to her lips and drank.

Nothing like the thin, sour Roman wine. This was warm. Complex. Cinnamon, clove, something sweet. Like warm figs. A warmth that had nothing to do with the alcohol spread through her chest.

"What is this?" she breathed, the question a gasp.

"A secret," he said, his voice dropping lower. "My own blend of spices. Imported from places far from here. Don't tell Gisco. He prefers his wine as he prefers all things: expensive, famous, and tasting of nothing."

A laugh bubbled up out of her. A real, deep, unrestrained laugh. The sound of it surprised her more than him.

His smile widened in response. As she looked at him—the scar, the confidence, the talk of spices—a name from the ship echoed in her mind: *Hanno. The silver-tongued serpent.*

"Lyrra! There you are."

Gisco's voice cut through the darkness, sharp and annoyed. *Bubble burst. Great. Back to the peacocks.* Revulsion washed over her at the thought of returning to his side, of feeling his proprietary hand on her arm.

Lyrra froze, handing the cup back to Hanno. "I must go," she whispered, the words tasting bitter in her mouth after the sweet wine.

She turned and hurried back toward the light of the doorway, not daring to look back, the taste of spice and a forbidden laugh still burning on her lips.

CHAPTER 7
A Private Reclamation

The morning light felt different. Warmer. Kinder. Lyrra lay in bed, the memory of the terrace a vivid, secret warmth against the cool morning air. His laugh. The taste of spice. The impossible, exhilarating feeling of being seen.

A soft knock preceded Asha's entry. She carried a tray with a small loaf of bread, a bowl of figs, and a cup of steaming mint tea.

"You're awake," Asha observed, setting the tray down. Her sharp eyes caught everything. "You have a strange look on your face. Like a cat that just found a secret bowl of cream."

Lyrra felt a blush creep up her neck. "I slept well."

"I'm sure you did," Asha said, a knowing smirk playing on her lips. "Gisco was asking after you. He wants to show you his prized collection of Iberian horses this afternoon. At least try to look interested." She paused at the door. "And my lady? That color of... contentment... on your face? It suits you."

The door clicked shut, leaving Lyrra alone in the sudden silence. Contentment. Was that what this was? This strange, light feeling in her limbs, something warm and restless. She replayed the moment on the terrace. The shared laugh. His eyes. The way he had seen her, not as an asset, but as a person.

She slipped out of bed, walked to the heavy wooden door, and slid the bolt firmly into place. The sound was a deep, definitive *thunk* that echoed in the quiet room. A wall between her and the world.

Returning to the bed, she pulled the sheer linen sheet up to her waist. The room was her sanctuary. The world—Gisco, his mother, the horses—was locked outside.

She closed her eyes, and his face materialized behind her lids. No, not Gisco's perfect features. This face... it had an easy smile. And a scar that made him real. The memory of his respectful gaze made something loosen in her body.

Her hands moved without permission, a slow, deliberate curiosity. This was her skin, her body. She traced the curve of her hip, her fingers feather-light over the tender flesh. *Stop. This is wrong*, a voice screamed in her head—her ingrained Roman upbringing. *But was it?* Her need was stronger. Her fingers drifted inward, across the flat plane of her stomach, down into the soft triangle of dark hair between her legs.

She hesitated, then pushed forward, parting the soft, slick folds. Her fingers, already wet with a moisture she hadn't known was there, found a small, hard knot of flesh. A jolt, sharp and electric, shot straight through her. Her breath hitched. That was it. That was the source.

Her clit.

The word, learned from the hushed, scandalized whispers of Roman matrons, felt alien and clinical in her mind. But the feeling it produced was anything but. She circled it gently. A low hum of pleasure started deep in her belly, a vibration that resonated through her bones. She pressed a little harder, and the hum intensified, her own wetness making her fingers glide. She was so wet for her own touch, for this illicit exploration. The scent of her arousal, musky and female, filled her senses, primal and intoxicating.

Another word came to her, one she'd heard spat as a vile insult. *Cunt.* Here, alone, slick with her own pleasure, it was not an insult. It was a place. A source. She whispered it to the empty room, tasting the taboo on her own tongue.

"My cunt."

The sound of her own voice saying the word sent a fresh shockwave of pleasure through her. She owned it. She moved her hips, a slow rocking, meeting the rhythm of her fingers. The pleasure was building now, tight and hot in her core, winding tighter. She wanted more. She picked up the pace, her fingers moving faster, harder, over her swollen clit. Gasps escaped her lips, small, desperate sounds. Her mind emptied of everything but the raw, building pleasure.

Hers.

Her back arched off the bed, her hips pushing desperately against her own hand. The spring snapped. A raw cry tore from her throat, a name she had only heard in temples, but one that felt right, powerful, female.

"Oh, Tanit! Yes!"

Her whole body went rigid, her inner muscles clenching and pulsing violently around nothing and everything as she came, a hot, pulsing flood that gushed over her fingers and down her thigh.

She lay there, shaking, boneless on the fur. Breath coming in gasps. No Roman guilt. No shame. *Should she feel shame?* She didn't know. Didn't care.

CHAPTER 8
The Serpent's Territory

This morning's invitation was a single, perfect saffron flower, laid beside her figs. *This was not Gisco's work.*

She glanced over at Asha, who offered no explanation, only a fleeting, conspiratorial glint in her eye. *Hanno.*

The message, planned by them in hushed whispers a night before, was clear. A taste of the world she'd glimpsed on the terrace. Attached was a tiny scrap of papyrus with a single symbol: a crescent moon. *Tonight.*

Her heart hammered against her ribs all day, quick and restless with a new, terrifying hope. When evening fell, Asha took charge. She arranged the pillows under the bedsheets to create the vague shape of a sleeping form. "A sudden headache," Asha coached, her face a mask of solemn concern. "The incense at the party. You require rest." It was a flimsy lie. They both knew it. Lyrra, for once, felt no guilt, only this thrilling anticipation that made her hands shake.

Cloaked in a servant's simple, dark wool, Lyrra slipped out a side entrance of the villa's garden. She met Hanno by a designated fountain in a quiet square, her pulse a frantic drum in her throat.

"I wasn't sure you'd come," he said.

"I wasn't sure either," she admitted, which made him smile.

He led her away from the grand, patrolled avenues and into the maze of the merchant quarter. The air here was different, thick with smells of leather, hot oil, and roasting nuts. He pointed out a stall where a man sold pyramids of ground spices—turmeric bright as gold, paprika red as sunset, cumin pale as desert dust.

Hanno tensed without warning. From the end of the alley, the rhythmic tramp of sandals on stone grew louder, with the familiar purple tint of Gisco's household guard.

He pulled her into the ink-black mouth of a doorway, his body a shield against the street. His chest was a wall of warmth at her back, his breath stirring the fine hairs on her neck as he whispered, "Stay still."

The guards passed, their voices fading. The alley was silent again, yet the small space thrummed with a new energy. Lyrra was acutely aware of everything: the hard muscle of his thighs pressed against the back of her legs, the strength in the hand that still rested on her arm, her own shallow breathing. He didn't move for a long moment. Neither did she. The tension was exquisite.

When he finally stepped back, the air rushed into her lungs, cool against her flushed skin. As they continued, Hanno's gaze fell on a man inspecting bolts of silk. His pace didn't falter. "Demetrios," he said, his voice suddenly flat and cool.

The man flinched. "Your new Tyrian purple is exquisite. I trust you enjoyed using my saffron profits to pay for it."

Demetrios went pale. "Hanno, I can explain—"

"No," Hanno cut in, his smile sharp and cold. "You can't. Come morning, your credit is dead. Your name is ruined. And I will still have my saffron." He didn't break stride, leaving the man shaking in his wake.

Lyrra stared after him, her heart pounding. The sailors had called him a silver-tongued serpent. She had just seen his venom. It was terrifying. And a part of her was thrilled by it.

He led her to a noisy tavern. Instead of taking a table, he guided her through the edge of the main room. As they moved a cheer went up from a group at the bar. A few men raised their mugs to Hanno. He gave a brief, almost imperceptible nod in return, his focus entirely on getting her through the crowd. Lyrra kept her head down, her hood pulled low, but her eyes shifted toward the source of the noise. Amidst the sailors and merchants, one face was familiar: Cato, one of Gisco's guards, grinning at them as he lifted his own cup.

Hanno pushed her quickly toward a beaded curtain. The private room beyond was a haze of smoke that smelled of cheap incense and stale wine. The low murmur of conversation at a round table cut off the moment the beads rattled shut behind them.

Two men looked up. One was built like a dock crane, dark-skinned and so still he seemed carved from stone. His silence was a presence in the room. The other was all sinew and sun-bleached hair, his eyes crinkling in a sailor's squint as they crawled over Lyrra, taking in every detail. A wry grin spread across his face as he leaned back in his chair.

"Gods, Hanno," he said. "You bring home a lot of strays, but this one looks expensive. Did you steal her from a temple?"

"Mago, this is Lyrra," Hanno said, ignoring the jibe. "Lyrra, this is Mago, who thinks he's funnier than he is, and Bomilcar, who has the good sense to keep quiet."

"So, 'Lyrra'," Mago said, leaning forward. "What's your story? Are you running from a husband or running toward a better one?"

"Perhaps I'm just running," she said, her voice clear and defiant.

Mago blinked, then let out a bark of laughter. He looked at Hanno and nodded with grudging approval. "I like her. Most runaways just look scared. She looks like she's ready to start a brawl or a fire." He took a long drink from his cup, then added casually, "Speaking of which, a trireme docked this morning. From Thera. The captain was asking after you. Said he was here on business for Telemon."

The name sucked the warmth from the room. The easy confidence vanished from Hanno's face. For a second, the man from the terrace was gone, and someone colder, sharper took his place. A stranger. He turned his head to Lyrra, his expression smoothing as her eyes met his.

He met her questioning look with a reassuring smile that didn't quite reach his eyes. "Telemon is an old… associate," he said, the word carrying a weight she didn't understand. He turned back to Mago, his voice level and firm. "Keep an eye out. I don't want any surprises."

Mago gave a curt nod, the humor gone from his face. Hanno then turned his full attention back to Lyrra, his smile becoming genuine again. But she had seen the shadow that crossed his face, and the warmth of his gaze couldn't erase the chill it left behind.

She took a breath, the air thick with smoke and stale wine. Surrounded by a sailor and a mercenary discussing a debt come due, she realized the frantic knot in her stomach had finally, impossibly, loosened.

CHAPTER 9
The Golden Collar

She had barely slept, but Lyrra was as bright as the risen sun. This morning's meal was an exercise in silent tension. Gisco, Sybil, and Lyrra sat at a long, polished cedar table in a sun-drenched atrium. The only sounds were the gentle splash of a nearby fountain and the soft clink of their cutlery. Lyrra felt exposed, examined, every breath measured.

"You seem... refreshed this morning, Lady Lyrra," Sybil observed, her voice cutting through the quiet sharp and cold. "I am pleased your headache has passed."

Lyrra merely nodded, her eyes fixed on the perfectly arranged figs on her plate. The lie from last night made her stomach clench.

A stroke of awareness traced a line down her neck. She didn't need to look up to know Gisco was watching her, his gaze a subtle, assessing weight over the rim of his cup. He was waiting.

He set down his cup. "I have something for you." He produced a flat box wrapped in deep purple velvet and slid it across the table. *Calculated. Rehearsed.*

Lyrra's hands trembled slightly as she opened it. Nested on a bed of white silk was a torc—a thick collar of woven gold. It was a masterpiece of Carthaginian filigree, intricate patterns swirling into a heavy, gleaming band. A hinge split the collar in half, allowing it to open like a jaw. The two ends were designed to connect around the throat, a perfect, inescapable circle. Her own throat felt tight just looking at it.

"It is exquisite," she breathed, because it was the truth, and because it was what she was expected to say.

"Only the finest gold, from the mines in Hispania," Gisco said with satisfaction, as if he'd personally dug it from the earth. "It befits the future matriarch of this house." He rose, moving behind her. "Let me."

Lyrra sat perfectly still as he lifted the heavy gold from its box. She flinched as the cold metal touched the back of her neck. *Heavy. So heavy.* He brought the two ends together with careful precision. The two ends met with a soft, definitive click. The sound seemed to echo in the silent room. Final. Permanent.

The weight settled on her collarbones. She fought the urge to touch it, to test the give of the clasp that sat cold against the nape of her neck. In her mind, she felt a phantom sensation: the light, warm pressure of Hanno's hand on her arm, protective and free.

"It suits you," Gisco said. He returned to his seat, a smug, satisfied smile on his face. His duty as a generous fiancé was done.

When the meal was finally over, Gisco and his mother departed for some meeting of state. Lyrra stood alone in the atrium, touching the torc despite herself. She stared at her reflection in a polished silver mirror, at the heavy gold collar that seemed to steal the very air from her lungs.

Asha entered quietly to clear the table. She stopped, walked around Lyrra, eyes narrowed.

"It is a masterpiece," she declared finally. Her voice dropped to a conspiratorial whisper. "You could probably buy a ship with it. *His* ship, preferably, and sail *him* far away from here."

CHAPTER 10
Her Own Coin

The torc was a near-permanent fixture now, its weight a constant pressure on her skin, on her spirit. She had to remind herself, often, that the weight was only metal. *Just metal. Not fate.*

One afternoon, she saw Asha in a corner of the kitchens, carefully folding scraps of exquisite Tyrian purple silk into a small pouch. Asha looked up, saw Lyrra's curious gaze, and hesitated before pulling the drawstring tight.

"A girl has to make her own way," Asha said with a shrug. "The off-cuts from the mistress's new tunic. A doll-maker in the market pays well for them." She tipped the pouch, and a few bronze coins clinked inside.

Lyrra looked from the coins to the scraps of silk, then back to her own hands. "I was taught to weave," she said, her voice low. "The patterns of my house are famously intricate. I could... help. I could weave the scraps into bands. They would be worth more."

Asha stared at her, her jaw slack with surprise. Then, a slow, delighted grin spread across her face. "Lady Lyrra, are you suggesting we go into business together?"

For the next week, they were co-conspirators. In the quiet hours of the afternoon, Lyrra would sit with Asha, noble fingers once trained for decorative tapestry, now working with a fierce, focused energy. They wove the silken scraps into beautiful, intricate bands, whispering and laughing like schoolgirls as they plotted their small, illicit enterprise.

When the work was done, Asha held out her hand. "Your share, my lady." She pressed three small bronze half-shekels into Lyrra's palm. They were warm from Asha's hand, worn with use. They felt heavier than all the gold stater in Gisco's villa. She closed her fist around them, a new and steady anchor in her palm.

The next day, their excursion to the market was a liberation. They walked with purpose, two businesswomen on a mission, surrounded by the sound of dozens of arguments over the price of fish and linen.

As they navigated the crowded lanes, Asha guided Lyrra toward a baker's stall, the air thick with the smell of warm bread. A young boy with flour dusting his dark hair grinned as they approached.

"Asha! My mother saved you the last of the salt biscuits," he said, holding out a small parcel wrapped in cloth. "She also said to tell you the ship *Nave de Cartago Nova* docked an hour ago. Came in on the early tide."

Asha's expression didn't change, but her eyes sharpened for a fraction of a second. "Did it now?" she said, her tone light. "Tell your mother she has my thanks, Bodash." She pressed a small coin into his hand.

As they walked away, she unwrapped a soft biscuit and offered half to Lyrra. "His mother served with mine in the old Hasherbalid house. We look after our own."

Lyrra took the offered half, a welcome contrast to the city's dust.

"That boy," Asha continued in a low voice, "runs deliveries for half the merchants in this quarter. Hears more than the High Priest's confessor, and he knows who his friends are." Her tone became even quieter, a lesson meant only for Lyrra. "Information, my lady. Give and take. The right word at the right time is sharper than any blade."

Lyrra's eyes scanned the stalls, past the spices and perfumes, until she found what she was looking for. It was a modest booth run by a quiet man who sold knives for fishermen and tools for leatherworkers. On a small velvet cloth lay a variety of fine blades.

Her eyes scanned past the brutish blades meant for soldiers. One blade stood apart. Slender and graceful, no longer than her hand. Small enough to be a secret. The hilt was simple, wrapped in worn leather, but the blade was polished steel, tapering to a point that looked elegantly dangerous. *Perfect.* Her pulse quickened just looking at it.

"How much?" she asked, her voice steady.

The craftsman named a price. Two bronze coins. Lyrra didn't haggle. She opened her fist and placed the coins on the counter. The man's eyes flickered over her, a brief, knowing look that took in the fine bones of her face despite the simple cloak. He said nothing, simply bit down on one of the coins to test its authenticity before scooping them up and handing her the dagger, wrapped in an oilskin cloth.

That night, she wore the golden torc to the evening meal, a perfect, smiling fiancée. Later, in the privacy of her room, she drew the dagger from its hiding place beneath a loose floor tile. One hand went to the cold, heavy gold at her throat. The other held the cool, light steel in her palm.

CHAPTER 11
The Festival of Tanit

"The Festival of Tanit?" Gisco scoffed, setting down his cup with a disdainful clink. "My dear Lyrra, that is a vulgar display for the lower classes. All that drumming and fire. A future matriarch of this house does not cavort with goat-herders under the moon." Lyrra looked at Asha, who stood silently by the door. A rebellious spark passed between them.

That evening, as Asha helped her fasten a simple, dark cloak over a plain tunic, they didn't speak. Asha's hands were steady as she worked the clasp. A look passed between them. It was enough.

"He'll be at the council meeting until late," Asha whispered, handing Lyrra a simple clay mask painted with the swirls of a crashing wave. "No one will know."

The festival was held in a large clearing outside the city walls. It was a wall of heat and noise. A dozen massive bonfires threw sparks at the moon, casting shadows that danced and shifted. The pounding of drums was primal, a pulse in the ground. An inescapable rhythm. Hundreds of masked figures circled the fires, their voices joined in a single, wild roar.

Behind the mask, she was just another body in the crowd. Not a Roman nobleman's daughter. Not Gisco's property. The thought was so new it was dizzying. She let the crowd pull her in.

And then she saw him.

He wore a mask carved like a hawk, but she knew his eyes. They found hers across the shifting, frenetic crowd with an impossible certainty, a magnetic pull. He made his way toward her, moving through the dancers with a smoothness that belied the chaos. He didn't speak. He simply held out his hand.

She took it.

They started with the slow, formal steps of the chant. A step, a turn. A careful space between their bodies.

Then the drums hammered faster. His hand found hers, his grip tightening. He pulled her closer, until the space was gone. His hand settled on the small of her back, warm through the thin tunic. The formal steps dissolved. Now they just moved together. His body guiding hers. Urgent. Wordless. She felt the strength in his arms. Saw the firelight dance in his eyes. Her skin flushed hot.

The drumming was a roar now. Deafening. He looked at her. A question in his eyes.

She gave a single, sharp nod.

He pulled her away from the firelight, out of the circle of dancers and into the shadows of an olive grove. He pressed her against the rough trunk of a tree. His mask was gone. The bark scraped through her cloak as his mouth came down on hers.

He tasted of spiced wine and woodsmoke. His hand moved to the nape of her neck, fingers twisting into her hair, pulling her impossibly closer.

A raw, desperate sound escaped her throat. Her hands fisted in the front of his tunic, pulling, trying to get closer. *More. I need more.* This heat, this living presence against her, was the answer to the cold weight that settled on her collarbones each morning. This was everything she craved.

When they finally broke apart, they were both breathless, their chests heaving, the air thick with the scent of their mingled desire.

"Lyrra," he whispered, his voice thick, a low rumble in the darkness, as if the name itself was a prayer he'd only just remembered. "I knew it was you."

CHAPTER 12

The Carthaginian Education

"Come with me," Hanno said, his voice a low plea in the moon-drenched quiet.

"Yes." The word left her lips before she could think, a single, explosive syllable of assent. There was no taking it back. She didn't want to.

He led her through the sleeping city, his hand a warm, constant presence in hers. They ended up at the port, before a large, dark warehouse that smelled faintly of cinnamon and salt. A side door led to a narrow staircase. At the top was his room.

It was nothing like Gisco's sterile palace. A large, simple bed dominated the space, covered in rough, soft furs. A massive map of the known world covered one wall. The air smelled of him. Sea and spice and something uniquely Hanno. The sound of the heavy iron bolt sliding home was a deep *thud*. A sanctuary.

He moved to her, his eyes dark with a desire that felt like a question, and kissed her. Her mouth opened under his, and the taste of him—wine and smoke and just *him*—went straight to her core. His hands moved on their own, finding the ties on her rough cloak.

And then her body betrayed her. A hard, fast flinch, an involuntary clenching of muscle that she couldn't control. *I've ruined it,* she thought, her stomach clenching into a hot, sour knot of shame.

He froze. His hands on her waist tightened, his knuckles turning white. "Did something happen?"

She looked down, unable to meet his eyes, but she could feel his hands trembling.

When she finally looked up, she saw a flash of something dangerous in his eyes, a murderous rage. *Was this for me?*

A jolt of terror shot through her. *Is he the same?*

But the anger wasn't aimed at her. It burned past her, aimed at the empty space in the room. At *him*.

The muscle in his jaw worked, a hard knot of control. His hands deliberately softened on her waist, and when he looked at her again, the stranger was gone. In his eyes was a look so tender it was almost a wound.

He gently tilted her chin, forcing her to meet his gaze. "That is not this. And I am not him." His thumb brushed a tear from her cheek. "We go at your speed. Only your speed. Do you understand?"

The words landed, and a wave of tearful relief washed over her. He wasn't just saying it. She had seen the rage in his eyes—not for her, but for what had been done to her. He had already proven it.

He moved to the simple knot of her cloak with deliberate care, a small, teasing smile playing on his lips. A shaky laugh escaped her as he let the heavy wool fall to the floor. He began on the ties of her tunic, his fingers gentle, his eyes never leaving hers.

When she stood before him in the moonlight from the window, she felt no shame, only the cool air on her skin. His breath caught, his gaze fixed on her as if seeing a sunrise for the first time.

Emboldened, she reached for the hem of his tunic. She explored the landscape of his body, the hard planes of his stomach, the map of scars. When she traced one particularly jagged line on his ribs, she felt his breath hitch, saw his eyes close for a moment. He was not just a legend. He was real. He had wounds, too.

She fumbled with the tie on his trousers. His hands covered hers, helping her undo the knot. He stepped out of them and stood naked before her. Unashamed. Magnificent.

A breath escaped her. Her gaze dropped. *Oh great.* A wave of dizzying panic and excitement pulsed through her. *The sailors weren't exaggerating about the 'Serpent' thing.*

He was… substantial. Intimidating. A creature of myth. Heat pooled low in her belly. *Gods.*

When she finally took him in her hand, a rough, uncontrolled groan tore from his throat, his hips bucking into her palm. A flash of pure power shot through her. *I did that. I can make this strong man weak.*

"My turn," he growled, his voice thick. He captured her hand, brought her knuckles to his lips, and kissed them. He knelt on the floor. Before her.

Her breath caught. *A man like that, on his knees. For me.* A thousand thoughts collided in her mind—this wasn't about submission. It was closer to worship.

He took her ankles, his grip firm but gentle, pulling her to the edge of the mattress. His thumbs stroked the arches of her feet, a small, unexpected touch that sent a shiver through her. He moved up, his lips brushing the inside of her knee, a touch so tender the screaming chorus of Roman shame in her head faltered, confused. He parted her legs. She felt his hot breath on her inner thigh a moment before he put his mouth on her.

Her first reaction was a jolt of pure shock, ingrained Roman shame. Her whole body went rigid, a reflexive instinct to close herself off. *This is for prostitutes. This is base.* But his hands moved to her hips, not to pin her, but to anchor her, a steady, grounding pressure. Then, there was only sensation. Overwhelming. Terrifyingly intimate. This was a territory she didn't even know existed.

She felt the broad, wet stroke of his tongue, a deliberate slide from bottom to top. It was a statement. A claim that was not about ownership, but about devotion. The shock was so profound it eclipsed the shame. He found that small, hard knot of flesh and went to work, his tongue a devastating, expert thing. He circled it, a slow, deliberate exploration that made the world narrow to a single point of heat. Then he used the flat of his tongue, applying a firm pressure that sent a low hum of pleasure vibrating through her.

The pleasure was so intense it was a form of annihilation, a warm tide that washed away every cold touch she had ever known, leaving only this. This heat. This focus. She felt his fingers, slick with her own wetness, slide inside her. To fill her, to stretch her, to give her something to grab on to while his mouth continued its relentless work. The feeling of being so full, of being taken so completely, shattered her last defense. A single, primal thought cut through the haze: *This is for me. Only for me.*

"Hanno!" she gasped, her voice breaking.

I heard myself scream his name.

Her fingers tangling in his hair, gripping him, anchoring herself to him as the pleasure began to build into a frantic, coiling serpent in her belly.

Her climax was a scream of release, not just of pleasure, but of the fear and shame she had been holding for so long. A breaking free. As the last tremor faded, she felt him swallow, a final, shocking act of acceptance that sent a fresh wave of tremors through her. She lay there, boneless on the furs, her body still trembling, utterly undone.

He moved up, crawling onto the bed beside her. Her eyes fluttered open. Dazed. He kissed her, a slow, deep press of his mouth to hers. The taste was shocking, intimate... It was the taste of herself. He had savored it.

He settled himself between her legs. The air was thick with the scent of them. Her legs parted for him, an unspoken invitation. He braced his hands on either side of her head, his body hovering over hers.

"Look at me, Lyrra," he whispered.

Her eyes snapped open and locked on his.

Slow. He pushed forward. An inch. She watched his face. His breath caught, but there was no fear in her. Just a wide, stunned awe. He pushed further. So tight. So hot. He set a rhythm. Slow. Measured. A steady, rocking beat.

Her hips, which had been still, started to move. A small, tentative rock at first, then a more confident rise to meet him. She felt the tension in his shoulders finally ease, a subtle, shuddering release of control. *He was waiting for me.*

Now she could let go.

He pulled her legs up, hooking them over his shoulders. The angle changed, burying him to the hilt. She cried out, a breathless sound of pure pleasure. That sound broke something in him, and the careful control was gone. His rhythm became a driving, pounding storm. But she wasn't afraid. She met the chaos with her own, her nails raking down his back, leaving trails of fire. Her hips slammed against his, her body bowing up from the bed. She felt the first tremors of her release begin, her muscles clenching around him, tighter and tighter.

She came with a scream, her back arched impossibly, her whole body convulsing around him, milking him, pulling at him. He drove into her one last time, a final, complete thrust, and roared as he poured himself into her.

He collapsed on top of her, his forehead pressed to hers, their breathing harsh and ragged in the quiet room. She felt the last pulses of his release deep inside her. Then, a strange stillness. The rhythm of his breathing changed, and a sudden, tense quiet fell over his body. A flicker of worry went through her. *Did I do something wrong?*

He lifted his head, his arms trembling with more than just exertion. She saw the worry in his eyes, a flicker of something she couldn't name, and then she saw it dissolve, replaced by a slow, reckless grin that felt dangerous and thrilling.

"Enjoying the Roman methods?" he whispered, his voice a low, teasing rasp.

The question was a relief, breaking the strange tension. A breathless, broken laugh escaped her. "They work," she gasped, a real smile touching her lips for the first time.

That smile, after everything, seemed to be a revelation for him. She saw something shift in his eyes—the dazed pleasure hardening into a sharp, intelligent curiosity. A flicker of daring.

"But," she said, her voice dropping to a whisper, "we're not in Rome."

The words hung in the air between them. An invitation. A challenge. His breath caught. Before he could find a response, she spoke again, her voice clearer now, though it still trembled.

"Show me," she whispered. "Show me *your* way."

"Turn around," he said, his voice a low growl, answering her call. "On all fours."

She saw the flash of her old Roman propriety warring with the new, wild thing she was becoming. Then, with a slow, deliberate grace, she moved. She positioned herself on her hands and knees on the furs, her back to him, her spine a straight, deliberate line of invitation.

His hand came down on her right cheek. Not hard. Just a sharp, open-palmed slap that made a satisfying *thwack* in the quiet room. The skin flushed red instantly.

She let out a sudden gasp and pushed back against his hand, a silent, hungry demand for more.

He settled behind her, his hands on her hips, his thumbs pressing into the soft flesh. He entered her with a single, powerful thrust. She cried out, a guttural moan as he filled her completely. This angle was different. Deeper. More primal.

He set a hard, driving rhythm, the sound of their bodies slapping together echoing in the quiet room. Obscene. Perfect. He gripped her hips, steering her, pulling her back onto him with every thrust. She met him, her own hips pushing back with a strength that stole her breath. This was a conversation.

"Gods, Lyrra," he growled into her ear, his voice hoarse. "Yes. Just like that."

He leaned forward, his chest pressed against her back, and wrapped one arm around her waist. His other hand slid down between her legs, his fingers finding her clit. It was already swollen, hard as a pearl. He circled it, rubbed it, matching the rhythm of his thrusts with the movement of his fingers.

She screamed, a primal, wordless cry of pure sensation. Her body bucked, her inner muscles clenching around him in a violent, pulsing rhythm. Her release tore his own from him. She felt him grip her hips, driving into her faster, deeper, as his own climax ripped through him, a hot, pulsing flood that felt like a brand of ownership—one she had willingly, eagerly chosen.

He collapsed against her back, his face buried in her hair. She felt him stay there for a long moment, the heavy, solid weight of him a comforting anchor. He pulled back, his movements gentle as he helped her turn onto her back. Her body was boneless on the furs, a wild mess of tangled hair and swollen lips.

He moved up her body and gathered her into his arms, pulling her against his chest. She made a soft, sleepy sound and curled into him, her head finding the hollow of his shoulder like it was made for her. Any tension she'd carried—in her neck, in her shoulders, in her soul—finally, impossibly, began to dissolve.

As sleep began to pull her under, a warm, heavy tide, she heard him whisper the words against her hair.

"Stay until sunrise."

It wasn't a command. It was a plea, full of a raw, aching need that sank into her as she finally let go.

CHAPTER 13
The New Shape of a Life

Lyrra woke to sunlight streaming through a high, dusty window. The air smelled of woodsmoke, spice, and him. She was curled against a hard, warm body, her head pillowed on his shoulder.

Her muscles ached—a deep, pleasant soreness in her thighs and lower back. She shifted, and a fresh warmth shot through her belly. A part of her brain, the Roman part, whispered shame. She quieted it.

Hanno stirred. His eyes opened, found hers. A slow smile spread across his face. "Sunrise," he murmured, his voice rough with sleep.

"It is," she said, not looking at the window.

He reached up, his thumb brushing her jaw. "Stay."

It wasn't a question or a command. It was a statement of a simple, undeniable fact: he wanted her here.

"I can't." The words were bitter in her mouth. *Gisco. The villa. Reality.* Cold and inevitable.

He didn't argue. Just nodded, his eyes holding hers. He kissed her gently, a soft meeting of mouths that felt less like an ending and more like a pause. They rose, dressing in the quiet room. He found a basket of dates and a jug of water. They ate and drank, sitting on the edge of the bed, their shoulders touching. The silence was comfortable, easy.

"So... how do we do this?" she asked, voicing the fear sitting heavy in her stomach.

"Carefully," he said, his expression serious. "We need a way to send messages."

They were quiet for a moment, thinking. Then, an image flashed in Lyrra's mind—Hanno in a tavern, sharing a laugh with a familiar face. "Cato!" she said, surprising them both. "He's a house guard at the villa. I've seen you with him."

Hanno's face lit up. "Cato," he breathed, pieces clicking into place. "Of course. We drink together some nights." He grinned. "The man loves to complain about his captain. He's perfect."

"Do you trust him?"

"With my life," Hanno said, his voice suddenly serious. He met her eyes. "And *you* are my life."

Cato would be their go-between. When had she become someone who sent secret messages to a lover? It gave her anxiety; it felt scandalous, even a little dramatic.

And yet... it felt right.

He walked her to a side alley near the villa, one that smelled of refuse and damp stone, a stark reminder of the world she had to return to. He kissed her one last time, deep and tasting of dates and promise. She'd remember this all day. "Go," he said, releasing her. "Be careful, Lyrra."

Lyrra slipped through the alley, her heart pounding a frantic rhythm against her ribs. She reached the back garden gate, which was unlocked as they had planned. Asha waited just inside, her face a mask of anxiety that dissolved into relief when she saw Lyrra.

"Gods, I thought you were caught!" Asha grabbed her arm, pulling her into the shadows of the garden wall. "Was your costume convincing?"

"It became less convincing as the night went on," Lyrra replied, and Asha snorted a laugh.

They crept through the garden, leaves wet with dew brushing against Lyrra's plain tunic. Back in her room, Asha helped her shed the disguise. She put on the familiar, opulent silks of her Carthaginian wardrobe. This fabric felt different now, binding against her newly awakened skin. She smoothed down the unfamiliar silk, fastening the intricate clasps, the heavy weight of the gold torc settling back onto her collarbones.

But as her gaze met her own in the gleaming silver of her vanity, her hands stilled. Her eyes, always downcast in Rome, were brighter, holding a spark she didn't recognize. Her lips, usually pressed into a thin line, were fuller, softer, a faint flush still lingering. There was a looseness to her shoulders, a subtle shift in her posture. The girl who had left Rome was a stranger now. *Would anyone else notice? Would Sybil's sharp eyes see the change?* A flood of fear washed through her. But the fear no longer smothered her fire; it fed it.

She had a secret now. And it was hers alone.

"Ready to face the peacocks?" Asha asked, her tone light.

Lyrra met her own eyes in her reflection. *Was she ready? Did she have a choice?*

"Ready," she said. The word felt like another lie. The voice that answered was hers, but it held a new resonance, a new power. Whether she was ready to fight for it... that remained to be seen.

CHAPTER 14
Practicing Living

A week passed. Days full of the formal rhythm of Gisco's villa. Lyrra wore the golden torc, smiled at the appropriate times, and navigated the polite, vicious games of Carthaginian high society. She played the part of the perfect fiancée well. But beneath all that silk and gold, the woman who had looked in the mirror remained. She walked differently now. Stronger. Her body felt like hers in a way it never had before.

The memory of Hanno was a secret ember she carried through the villa's cold halls. She was living two lives. Her performance in the villa's walls should have been exhausting. But the secret wasn't a burden; it was a shield. A hidden weapon.

Her thoughts often returned to his room, to the scent of him, to his skin against hers. But more than that, she kept thinking about herself. The spark she had ignited that morning, alone in her bed, had not gone out.

Nearly every night, in the quiet of her chambers, she fanned that flame. Her own hands, retracing the path Hanno had shown her, learning the difference between a frantic, clumsy trial-and-error and a slow, deliberate pressure that made her breath stagger. She learned the rhythm that led to her release, the way her own muscles would clench and pulse in the aftermath.

One early afternoon, Lyrra sat in the central atrium, carefully embroidering a cushion.

"You know, the walls in this villa?" Asha said, breaking the silence from across the room. She was folding one of Sybil's sheer tunics with unnecessary force. "They're thinner than a prostitute's self-respect."

Lyrra froze, a blush creeping up her neck. "Seriously?"

Asha met her eyes, a wicked glint shining in them. "Oh, yes. Tanit and the gods must have been answering someone's very fervent prayers the other night." She paused, grinning. "From somewhere near your chambers, perhaps?"

Lyrra's face was hot now, but a laugh escaped her lips, free and clear. "Asha! You listen at doors?"

"Nooo…" Asha grinned. "I said the walls are thin, my lady. And it's only for entertainment," she replied with a shrug. "This place can be terribly dull otherwise. Though," she added, softening, lips starting to curl, "I was glad to hear you sounded so, *well*, the other day." Asha's smirk was infectious. Lyrra met her gaze, and a shared, boisterous laugh erupted between them, echoing through the villa.

CHAPTER 15
An Offering to the Dead

The next opportunity to meet up with him came two days later.

A sharp moment of clapping called the household staff together. Asha, three other attendants, and two off duty house guards gathered in the central atrium, their faces blank with practiced obedience. Curious and unsure of her place, Lyrra stood among them, a new kind of tension coiling in her gut.

Sybil stood at the foot of the grand staircase as they began to gather. She ascended halfway up the staircase, stopping there to ensure she physically rose above the assembled staff. Looking down at them, her expression was cool, imperious, a mask of stone.

"Gisco and I have received a lovely invitation," Sybil announced, her voice cutting through the quiet hall. Clear, precise. Gloating. "A banquet at Senator Hamilcar's estate. We will be attending tonight." She paused, her gaze sweeping over the staff. Satisfaction flashed across her face. Superiority. "It is expected to last until sunrise. Make the necessary preparations."

Sybil stood there for a moment, her eyes narrowed, waiting. The expected chorus of "Yes, my lady" never came. The staff simply waited, silent. Sybil's lips thinned almost imperceptibly. "You are dismissed," her voice tight as she waved them away.

It was a simple, quick announcement. Sybil turned to sweep up the remaining stairs, her silks whispering with disdain against the stone steps.

Until sunrise. Lyrra's mind seized on the words. An entire night. The villa would be mostly empty, only a couple weary house guards on duty. A chance. The thought sent a thrill through her, sharp and electric. She was dead set on making this work for her. For them.

o o o o o

Later that evening, Lyrra found Asha in the kitchens, calmly portioning out the evening meals for the household guards. Lyrra's target was the meal tray of Cato, the off-duty guard she'd once seen sharing a laugh with Hanno in a smoky tavern. Hanno said he trusted him with his life. That was good enough for her. He was now their mule, whether he knew it or not.

Lyrra approached the bustling countertop, her movements casual. She picked up a warm, flat bread destined for Cato's tray. With a fingertip, she scooped a tiny amount of turmeric paste from a bowl and, shielding her action from the other kitchen staff, quickly smudged a lopsided, golden-yellow heart onto the bread's surface.

Asha, who missed nothing, paused. A sly, teasing smile touched her lips. "Oh?" she murmured, her voice a low whisper. "Expanding your collection, my lady? I didn't realize Cato was on the list."

Lyrra's head snapped up, her cheeks flushing. "Asha! Gods, no! He's… unpleasant."

"I agree," Asha said, her eyes twinkling. She glanced from Lyrra's flustered face to the turmeric heart. The teasing smile on her lips slowly replaced by dawning admiration. "Ah," she said softly. "So the message isn't for the mule. It's for the man he drinks with." She gave Lyrra a subtle, deliberate wink.

Lyrra let out a breath she didn't realize she'd been holding. It was useless trying to hide anything from Asha. She simply nodded.

"The Punic tombs again?" Asha asked, already knowing the answer.

Lyrra felt a fresh wave of surprise. "How do you...?"

"My lady," Asha said, turning back to her work with an air of finality. "I see everything that happens in this house. Now. Why the obsession with that dusty old place?"

Lyrra found herself confessing in a whisper, "I don't know... It's quiet. Dark. Peaceful. It feels like the only place in this city that isn't trying to sell me something."

Asha snorted softly, placing the last of the vegetables on Cato's tray. "Nothing says 'I'm desperately in love' like a romantic evening surrounded by ancient dead people. Very well. I'll make sure Cato gets his... love note." She pushed the tray toward a waiting servant. "Go. Get ready. And try not to get caught this time."

o   o   o   o   o

With Gisco and Sybil gone, the villa felt like a different world—peaceful and quiet. Getting out was a matter of moving like a ghost through the familiar corridors, every shadow a potential witness.

She slipped out a side gate into the cool night air. Her cloak was a welcome shield of anonymity as she walked quickly and intentionally with his face in her mind.

She reached the Punic tombs first, a lone figure in the pale moonlight. She found a spot to wait, leaning against the cold, rough stone of a mausoleum, the silence of the dead a strange comfort.

Moments passed. Her mind wandered. She felt the familiar weight of the pendant in her pocket.

She pulled it out. The gold was cold against her skin, Juno's face a stony, silent judgment. *Marriage. Duty. Not like this.*

It had been her reminder of a time before Gisco. Now, with Hanno, with this wild, living pulse in her veins, the pendant was an anchor. A chain.

With a sigh, she decided to put it away. It was too much to think about right now. She lifted the edge of her cloak, her fingers fumbling in the dark to find the small, hidden inner pocket. She was pushing the fabric aside, searching for the seam…

A hand clamped on her waist. She gasped, spinning around.

It was Hanno. His mouth was on hers before she could make a sound, a deep, hungry kiss that stole the air from her lungs. Startled, her hands flew up, her arms wrapping around his neck to steady herself, her fingers digging into the strong muscles of his shoulders. She answered his kiss with her own, a desperate, affirming pressure.

A man's shout echoed from the far end of the necropolis. A guard's laugh followed.

Hanno broke the kiss instantly, his body going tense. "Come on," he whispered against her ear. He grabbed her hand and pulled her away, deeper into the maze of shadows, until they found a more secluded alcove, hidden between two crumbling mausoleums. The voices faded. The danger passed, but the adrenaline still sang in her veins.

"You're early," he murmured, pressing her back against the stone, his body caging hers.

"You're late," she countered, her hands sliding from his shoulders down his chest, feeling the frantic beat of his heart.

The kiss that followed was slower. Deeper. The frantic edge was gone, replaced by something else. An exploration. He was mapping her mouth with his, learning the shape of her, and she was learning him right back.

His hand slid under her cloak, the rough wool scraping against her arm. It found her breast. Even through the fabric of her tunic, the heat of his palm was a brand. His thumb found her nipple, rubbing, a slow, deliberate circle, and a jolt went straight down, deep inside her. She gasped into his mouth, the sound swallowed by his.

It was her turn.

Her hands slid from his shoulders, down the hard wall of his chest. She could feel the frantic beat of his heart under her palm. *Thump-thump-thump.* A match to her own. Down, over the tense muscle of his stomach. She wanted to know all of him. Her hand found him through the thin linen of his trousers. *Hard. Gods, he was so hard.* And getting harder for her. The thought was a dizzying, intoxicating poison.

She wrapped her fingers around him, the thick ridge of his cock a solid, living thing in her hand. He groaned, a raw sound against her ear, and pushed himself into her grip. *Yes. That was the sound I wanted.* The sound of him wanting her. The sound of him losing himself to her.

He was giving himself over to her touch, and she was taking everything.

She started to move her hips, a slow grind against his, her hand still stroking him through the fabric, feeling the damp heat build between them. He mirrored the movement, his own hips pressing back, chasing the friction.

His other hand slid down her back, under the cloak, and cupped her ass, fingers digging in, pulling her tight against him. So tight she could feel the exact shape of his cock against her belly. A desperate, clumsy dance with too many clothes in the way. She wanted to tear them off. She wanted to feel his skin on hers.

He tore his mouth from mine, both of us panting, our breath fogging in the cool night air. His forehead rested against mine.

"Gods, Lyrra," he rasped, his voice wrecked. "If we don't stop..."

He didn't have to finish. She knew. The fire was too hot; it would burn them both down right here if they let it. She nodded, her own breath coming in ragged gasps.

But she didn't let go. Not yet. She kept her hand right where it was, holding him, feeling the last of his tremors beneath her palm.

He took her hand—the one still pressed against him—and gently pulled it away. But he didn't let go. He brought her hand to his lips and kissed her knuckles, his eyes never leaving hers in the moonlight.

The fire was still there, a low burn in her belly, but something else surfaced with it. A different kind of hunger, one that had nothing to do with skin. She also wanted his day. She wanted his frustrations. She wanted the boring, mundane pieces of his life because they were his. She wanted to know the man who lived in the world outside of these stolen, frantic moments in the dark.

She pulled back just enough to breathe. "Tell me something," she whispered. "Something real. What did you do today?"

The question seemed to surprise him. "I argued with an import official for three hours over a shipment of Egyptian linen," he said, his voice a low rumble against her forehead. "He has a face like a pug and the mind of a particularly slow goat."

She let out a real laugh, the sound muffled against his chest. "I listened to Sybil complain that the new batch of wine from Hispania is 'too aggressive' for the evening meal."

"Gods, we're a pair," he said, but he was smiling. He kissed her again, a long, lingering kiss that spoke of shared frustration and the simple relief of being together. Of being seen. They didn't speak of plans or conspiracies. They just held each other in the dark, two people stealing a moment of life from the tombs that surrounded them.

They parted as the moon began its slow descent. One last, hard kiss—a taste of rain and resolve. Then he was gone.

Lyrra crept back through the garden alone. She was her own keeper now. Safe in her room, she shed the cloak, her mind replaying every touch, every word.

CHAPTER 16
The Quiet Command

The warmth of the previous night, of Hanno's arms around her in the moonlit dark, felt a world away. It was a secret ember she held in her chest, a tiny point of heat against the cold of the villa. But the memory was not enough to warm her now.

The source of the chill was Gisco. He had spent the morning striding through the atrium, recounting his latest business triumph to a pair of visiting merchants. His voice, loud and self-satisfied, echoed from the stone floors, a constant, grating reminder of his power.

Lyrra, forced to sit with Sybil and listen, felt a familiar, quiet fury building in her chest. She needed to escape before the heat of it showed on her face. Excusing herself with a murmur about the heat, she sought refuge.

She found it in a small antechamber off the main corridor, where the household silver was kept. Asha was there, her back to the door, methodically polishing a large ewer. The repetitive, rhythmic scrape of cloth against metal was a balm. Lyrra walked to the long table, picked up a soft linen cloth and a simple wine goblet, and began to work. She didn't need to speak. The shared, mundane task was its own kind of conversation.

After a few moments of silence, Asha held up the piece she'd been cleaning. It was a salt cellar of absurd design, a silver dolphin locked in a desperate, writhing struggle with a many-tentacled squid. She squinted at it.

"The mistress Sybil says this represents the triumph of Carthaginian commerce over the chaos of the sea," Asha murmured, her voice a low, conspiratorial hum. She paused, rubbing a stubborn tarnish spot on one of the squid's arms. "I think it represents a man with too much money who'd never been on a real boat. The squid is winning."

A small, choked laugh escaped Lyrra's lips, sharp and unexpected. The sound broke the dam of her composure. "He's insufferable today."

"He learned it from her," Asha said simply, not looking up from her work. "Gisco shouts so you know he's a wolf. Sybil purrs so you forget she's a panther until she strikes."

Lyrra stopped polishing. She stared at the warped reflection of her own face in the curve of the goblet, the silver distorting her features. *A panther.* The prison she inhabited suddenly felt infinitely more complex, its bars built by a quiet, unseen architect.

Their task finished, Asha stacked the polished silver. "Come," she said. "The guest wing needs fresh linens."

As they walked through the silent, cavernous corridors, their arms laden with folded linen, Asha nodded toward a vast mosaic that dominated one wall. It depicted a naval victory, ships with purple sails sinking a rival fleet.

"Gisco's grand triumph," Asha said, her voice barely a whisper. "Paid for by a 'shipping loss' so catastrophic the sea itself must have swallowed the gold. Funny how the sea was kind enough to spit the exact amount back into the mosaicist's purse. The gods are generous with their accounting when Sybil is the one making the prayers."

As they continued down a less-trafficked corridor, Asha paused beside a heavy tapestry depicting a hunting scene. She lifted the thick, dusty wool, revealing not a stone wall, but a narrow, rough-hewn wooden door set almost flush against the mortar. The air that drifted out was cool and smelled of stone.

"The servant passages," Asha whispered, letting the tapestry fall back into place with a soft thud. "So we can move through the house like ghosts. Useful, but unseen." Her voice was laced with a familiar, bitter humor. "They hide the doors behind the art, so the masters can pretend the house runs itself."

As they navigated back into the main corridor, a nervous-looking scribe scurried out of Sybil's private study, his arms full of scrolls. He nearly collided with them, stammering an apology before hurrying on his way.

"Isn't that Marcus?" Lyrra asked. "Gisco's man?"

"He is," Asha confirmed. "But Gisco pays his salary. Sybil pays his gambling debts. Who do you think gets the honest report?"

Lyrra stopped walking, the weight of the linens in her arms suddenly forgotten. The boasting, the whispers of 'misfortune', the quiet control. It all fit. "So... Gisco is just a... a figurehead?"

Asha met her gaze, her dark eyes serious. "He's the face on the coin. She's the hand in the treasury. He's the barking dog; she holds the leash."

They arrived in Lyrra's chambers. Lyrra dropped the linens on a chair and sank onto the edge of her bed, her mind reeling. The enemy wasn't just the arrogant man she was supposed to marry. It was his quiet, smiling mother. The walls of her prison, which she had thought were made of Gisco's ego, were in fact built from Sybil's cold, calculating ambition. They were higher, thicker, and more intelligently designed than she had ever imagined.

"She controls everything," Lyrra whispered, the words barely audible, spoken more to herself than to Asha. "The money, the men... everything. How can anyone hope to ever escape that?"

Asha stood before her, her posture rigid. The usual wit was gone from her face, replaced by a hard, cold memory. "My mother," she said, her voice low and flat, "served in the house of the Hasherbalids before she came here. One night, the master's son— a boy with cruel hands and a fouler mouth—cornered her in the kitchens. She fought back. Broke his nose with a wine jug."

Asha's eyes locked with Lyrra's. "They didn't sell her. They flogged her in the courtyard as an example. She never walked without a limp again. Gisco is just like him, Lyrra. Polished marble on the outside, rotten underneath. They think because they own the house, they own everyone in it. They think we won't do anything about it."

Lyrra's hands were trembling. She clenched them into fists, nails digging into her palms. The sting was a welcome, grounding pain. She looked at Asha, truly seeing her for the first time—not as a handmaiden, but as another woman trapped in the same cell. And in the pit of her stomach, where the numbing dread had been, something new and dangerous began to uncoil.

The heavy silence was finally broken by Asha letting out a long, weary sigh, her pragmatic humor returning like a familiar shield. "So," she said. "We just have to ruin the most powerful woman in Carthage. No trouble at all."

She leaned in, her voice a low, conspiratorial rasp. "That's the facade. He gets to be the prick running his mouth. She's just the asshole." She paused, a flash of pure contempt in her eyes. "Doing asshole things."

She walked over to the corner of the room and nudged a loose floor tile with her toe. "We should start by hiding your dagger somewhere better than this. Even Gisco might find that, and he can barely find his own dick in the morning."

A raw, startled laugh escaped Lyrra's lips, cutting through her fear. The sound was a relief, a small pocket of air in a room that was quickly running out of it. She rose from the bed, her resolve hardening into something new.

"Where?" Lyrra asked, her voice steady now.

Asha's eyes scanned the opulent room, dismissing the obvious places—beneath the mattress, inside a chest. Her gaze landed on a heavy, ornate tapestry depicting a Roman hunting scene.

"There," Asha said, pointing. "Behind the boar."

Together, they lifted the heavy wool. The wall behind it was rough-hewn stone. Asha ran her fingers along the mortar until she found a loose section. With a bit of wiggling, she worked a stone free, revealing a small, dark cavity within the wall.

Lyrra retrieved the dagger from beneath the floor tile. The cool leather of the hilt felt different in her hand now—not just a tool for escape, but a shared secret. She placed it inside the hollow space. They fit the stone back into place, and when they let the tapestry fall, the hiding spot vanished completely.

The dagger was safe. The secret was theirs.

CHAPTER 17
A Calm Promise of Ruin

The evening meal stretched into the deep of the night. Gisco, playing the part of the magnanimous host, was in his element. He kept the wine flowing for the visiting magistrate, a portly man from Numidia named Cassius, whose face grew redder with every cup. Dessert was skipped entirely. "The sweetest fruit," Gisco declared with a predatory smile, "is a deal well-struck."

Lyrra watched him, a knot of ice in her stomach. This was the performance Asha had described. Gisco wasn't just a host; he was a hunter, patiently intoxicating his prey. He drank little himself, his eyes remaining sharp and clear as he steered the conversation from pleasantries to the price of grain. He spoke of a rival's recent "misfortune"—a shipment lost to a sudden storm off the coast of Sicily.

"A terrible tragedy," Gisco said, his tone smooth. "He's had to sell his holdings in the silver mines to cover the loss. I, of course, offered him a fair price. One must support one's friends in their time of need."

Lyrra felt a chill that had nothing to do with the cool marble hall. She felt certain that Sybil had orchestrated the "storm" that sank the man's fortunes. Sybil sat at the far end of the table, silent and observant, a serene smile on her face. Like watching a play she had written, pleased with her lead actor's performance.

Finally, the magistrate, his wits softened by wine and his pockets lightened by a deal he would regret in the morning, was escorted out. The moment the great doors closed, the warmth vanished from the hall. The servants moved with silent efficiency to clear the table.

Sybil rose. She glided down the length of the table to her son. She placed her hands on Gisco's shoulders, a gesture that looked maternal but felt proprietary. As she straightened, her eyes met Lyrra's across the room. The look was brief, sharp, and utterly unreadable. Then she turned and swept out of the hall.

Lyrra stood and turned to leave, brushing down the wrinkles and folds of her stola. Her only thought was the quiet of her own chambers. She had taken three steps toward the corridor when his voice cut through the quiet. It was not loud, but it stopped her dead.

"A word, Lyrra."

She turned slowly. He hadn't moved. He was just watching her, the sense of his mother's touch still on his shoulder.

"In my study."

It wasn't a request. Every step she took toward the study at the end of the long, shadowed corridor, felt heavier than the last. Her mind was terrifyingly clear.

He led the way down the long, shadowed corridor, his footsteps silent on the mosaic floors. Lyrra followed, the space between them charged with a silent, unnerving tension. He stopped before the heavy cedar door of his study, pushed it open, and stood aside, gesturing for her to enter.

She stepped past him into the room.

The door closed behind her with a solid, final *thud*. Darkness swallowed her. Her eyes strained, the only light, a tiny, sputtering orange flame from an oil lamp on a distant desk. It was set too low to illuminate anything but itself. The air was still and cool on her skin.

He moved past her silently, a shape in the oppressive dark sweeping past the wall of scrolls receding into darkness.

"A beautiful night," he said, his voice a disembodied sound in the darkness. "Clear enough to see the stars."

Lyrra's heart began a slow, heavy drum against her ribs. She stood frozen just inside the door, a statue carved from fear, her eyes struggling to adjust.

He walked to his desk, the soft scrape of his sandals on the stone, then silence. She saw his hand, a pale shape, reach for the lamp and adjust the wick. The flame caught, bloomed, and pushed the deep shadows back to the corners of the room.

The room revealed itself in stages. First, the polished surface of the desk, then the neat rows of scrolls lining the walls behind him, testaments to his family's power. Finally, the light washed up over him. It caught him from below, carving sharp, unnatural hollows into his face—it was composed, almost casual. Unrushed.

"The tombs are a beautiful part of our city's heritage," he said, his voice calm, conversational. "A reminder of what lasts."

Lyrra's heart began a slow, heavy drum against her ribs. She said nothing, her throat too tight to form words.

"And prayer," he continued, "is so important for a woman's character. It teaches piety. Humility. And discretion."

He straightened a stack of papyrus. He adjusted the wick of the lamp, making the flame burn a fraction brighter. He was making her wait.

Finally, he held out his hand, fingers closed around a small object. He released his grip. Slipping down on a thin gold chain, an oval of glass and gold bounced and dangled.

It was her father's pendant.

The room tilted. It was smaller now. Tighter. Her clothes were tight. Her lungs were tight. Her face flush and hot. Her ears rang so loud she could barely hear his next words.

Gisco adjusted his outstretched arm to hold the pendant up to the flame, the light filtering through the detailed cameo. "A groundskeeper found this," he said, his voice unnervingly level. "He brought it to my mother."

He let that statement hang in the air.

"She was also concerned," Gisco went on, his eyes finally meeting Lyrra's. They were as flat and lifeless as stone. "Not that you were praying, of course. We all encourage piety. But that your prayers seem to require such… company."

Company? Does he know? How? Did someone see us? Oh gods, Hanno.

His gaze flickered down to the pendant he now held loosely in his hand. "And that they take place in a dusty, common tomb instead of a proper temple."

Lyrra's jaw tightened, a barely perceptible clench of muscle. She forced it to relax. Her voice was a choked whisper. "I… I don't know what you mean."

He took a step toward her, a small, knowing smile playing on his lips. "Don't you? The groundskeeper who found your pendant has a loose tongue. He mentioned seeing a man with a distinctive cloak near the tombs that same night. A coincidence, I'm sure."

He sighed, a theatrical sound of disappointment, and walked back to the desk. "A Roman noblewoman meeting secretly in the dark. It's a bit… common. I would have thought if you were to seek out 'local flavor', you would have chosen better than a back-alley spice merchant." He tossed the pendant onto the polished wood. It landed with a sharp, definitive clink.

Spice merchant. He said it. It's not a guess. He knows exactly who. Asha's warnings—it's all true. He sees everything.

"Honestly, Lyrra, that's what disappoints me the most. Not the infidelity. That's boring. It's the sheer lack of imagination. Him? He deals in fleeting pleasures, in scents that fade. I deal in permanence. In gold. In ships. In power. You made a bad trade."

He leaned against the desk, crossing his arms, his posture still maddeningly casual. "So let's be clear," he said, his voice now flat, cold, and final. "I am not a jealous man. Jealousy is a vulgar emotion for lesser men. It implies a lack of control."

He paced the room slowly, his hands clasped behind his back. "I am, however, a businessman. And you, my dear, are a recent and very significant acquisition. An investment in the future of my house. Your purpose is to provide stability, an heir, and a flawless public image. You have, it seems, failed to grasp the fundamentals of your role."

Acquisition? Investment? This is about property rights. And I am the property.

He stopped, turning to face her. His eyes were devoid of any emotion at all. "The spice merchant. Hanno. A romantic, if predictable, choice. He deals in fleeting pleasures. I deal in permanence."

"You don't know anything," she said, her voice trembling slightly. She wanted to run. *She would've run.* But not now.

"Oh, but I do," Gisco countered. He turned away from her and walked to the high, narrow window, gazing out at the scattered lights of the sleeping city below. His voice was calm, conversational, as if he were merely commenting on the view.

"I know he owns three ships: the *Star of Tyre*, the *Desert Wind*, and the *Sea Nymph*." He spoke, his back still to her. "I know he owes a considerable sum to a moneylender in Alexandria. I know his most profitable trading partner is a man named Phares in Utica, a man who also happens to be deeply in my family's debt. And, of course, he's actively being sought out by Telemon of Thera." He turned back and caught her eyes in his gaze. "A man not known for his patience."

The level of detail hit her like a punch. She couldn't breathe.

"You *will not* touch him," she whispered, the words a desperate plea.

Gisco laughed. Not with amusement. Dismissal. "Touch him? Gods, no. That would be messy. Vulgar. Unbecoming."

He stepped closer, his voice dropping to a confidential, conspiratorial hush, the sound more terrifying than any shout. "No, Lyrra. This is what will happen. I will have a quiet word with Phares in Utica, who will abruptly cancel his contracts. The moneylender in Alexandria will suddenly, and with great regret, call in Hanno's debt, all of it, immediately. His ships will be seized as collateral. His dockside warehouse, which is leased, will have its lease terminated. His crew, Mago and the rest, will be blacklisted from every port between here and Egypt. He will be ruined. A beggar in the streets he once walked like a king. And everyone, everyone, will know that he tried to touch what belongs to Gisco, and that this is the price."

He paused, letting the words sink in, the words settling like lead in her stomach. "I will not lay a hand on him. I will simply... erase him. By this time next month, the name 'Hanno' will be a cautionary tale whispered by old women. A ghost."

He reached out and gently, almost tenderly, touched the golden torc at her neck. His fingers felt cold against her skin.

"You will be my wife," he said, his voice quiet and final. "You will smile at my side. You will bear my children. And you will watch from the window of this villa as the world forgets he ever existed. This is not a threat. It is the new shape of your life. Accept it."

He turned and walked back to his desk, picking up a scroll as if their conversation was already over, a minor piece of household administration now concluded.

Lyrra stood frozen in the center of the room. He had dismissed her without a word. She turned, her movements stiff, and walked out of the study. The journey back down the long corridor was a walk through a waking nightmare. Everything—the intricate mosaics, the shimmering silks hanging on the walls, the polished floors—blurred together into a smear of opulent color that was suffocating her.

CHAPTER 18
The Unbreakable Promise

Lyrra did not cry. Tears were a luxury, a release, and Gisco had left no room in her for anything but a vast, bottomless dread. By the time she reached her chambers, the fire in her chest, the one that had sparked her rebellion, was gone. She sat on the edge of her bed, the heavy gold torc a dead weight on her collarbones, and felt nothing. A tomb of her own. Trapped. Utterly and completely.

Gisco's words echoed in the silence of the room. *I will simply... erase him.* Not with a sword, but with a scroll. With a whispered word in a moneylender's ear. With the casual, devastating power she had never truly understood until now.

Do I submit to him? It would be easy. So easy. Become the beautiful, vacant wife he wanted. A perfect Roman statue. She would smile at his parties, bear his sons, and in time, the memory of Hanno—of spice, and laughter, and the feel of his hand on her back—would fade. It would become a ghost, just as he would. A quiet, painless, living death.

Then, she caught her reflection in the mirror across the room. She saw a woman with haunted eyes, her shoulders slumped in defeat. A woman already turning hollow. Revulsion hit her and cut through the numb despair.

No.

The word was a silent scream in her mind. She thought of Hanno's thumb on her jaw. His voice in the dark. Her own body coming alive under her own hands. That raw cry she'd given to her goddess. That was life. That was real. Gisco was offering her a beautiful grave.

She straightened her spine, her hands clenching into fists at her sides. The fear was still there, her stomach clenched tight, but beneath it, something else was stirring. That rage from the alley in Rome. Still there, still burning.

The prison wasn't the villa. Wasn't even the gold at her throat. The prison was his power. His influence. His network of debts and favors across the Mediterranean.

You don't escape a cell like that.

You break it.

The thought was so simple it stole the air from her lungs. Running away was surrender. It meant Gisco won. It meant Hanno was still ruined, a ghost haunting the life she had salvaged. To save him—to save herself—she couldn't just flee. She had to tear down Gisco's power from the inside.

She walked to the heavy tapestry of the boar hunt, shifting the loose stone behind it. Her fingers found the cold, hard steel of the dagger. She drew it out. The weight felt familiar, comforting. A tool for prying things open. For leverage.

But to utterly destroy Gisco, she needed more than a blade.

She needed an ally.

She walked to the bell pull, the dagger still clutched in her hand, hidden in the folds of her tunic. Her movements were calm now, deliberate. She pulled the cord.

When the servant appeared at the door, Lyrra's voice was steady and level with authority.

"Send Asha to me. Now."

CHAPTER 19
Righteous Treason

The knock on the chamber door was soft, hesitant. Asha entered to find Lyrra standing by the window, dark against the lingering evening. The room was still, tension thick. Asha's eyes darted around, looking for signs of distress, for tears or hysterics. She found none. Instead—a cold, unnerving stillness in her mistress that was more frightening than any outburst.

"My lady?" Asha began, her voice cautious. "You sent for me?"

Lyrra turned from the window. "Yes." Her face was pale, her expression unreadable. She walked past Asha to the heavy chamber door and slid the bolt home with a dull sound in the quiet room. She walked to the small table in the center of the room and sat. She gestured for Asha to do the same.

Asha hesitated, then perched on the edge of the other chair. "Is everything… alright?"

"No," Lyrra said, her voice flat, devoid of emotion. "Gisco knows about Hanno."

The blood drained from Asha's face. Her usual bravado vanished, replaced by raw fear. "Gods," she breathed, her hands flying to her mouth. "How? What did he say? What is he going to do?"

"He's going to destroy everything," Lyrra answered. She then recounted Gisco's promise, not as a panicked victim, but as a general relaying an enemy's battle plan. She detailed the cancelled contracts, the called-in debts, the blacklisting. The whole plan to destroy Hanno. Her voice never wavered.

When she finished, Asha was shaking her head, her eyes wide with terror. "We have to warn him. He has to run. He has to get on a ship and never come back."

"And go where?" Lyrra countered, her voice sharp. "Gisco's reach is long. He would be a beggar in any port in this sea. Running is a death sentence. Maybe a slow one, but a death sentence nonetheless."

"Then what?" Asha whispered, her voice desperate. "There is nothing to be done. He is the most powerful man in this city, after the council itself. Fighting him is impossible."

"Then we find a way to fight back." Lyrra leaned forward, meeting Asha's eyes. "He wants to erase Hanno. Destroy my future. Own me. I won't let that happen. I'll destroy him first."

Asha stared at her as if she had sprouted a second head. "Are you mad? You? A Roman girl who has been here, what, a month? How do you propose you do that?"

"With you," Lyrra said. "He uses money and information as his weapons. We will use them as ours. He is insulated by his power, but he's not a god. He has weaknesses. We just have to find them."

Asha's cynical humor was gone. In its place was a stark, unnerving stillness. Lyrra's gaze dropped to Asha's hand on her knee. It was trembling. Asha saw her looking and quickly clenched it into a fist.

"This is treason," Asha whispered. The word landed like a stone, sucking the air from the room.

Lyrra didn't flinch. She held Asha's fearful gaze. "Then it's a treason worth committing. He would destroy an innocent man for his pride. There's no honor in serving a man like that."

The fear on Asha's face didn't vanish. It hardened into something else. Something sharp and calculating. She leaned forward. "Alright, my lady," she breathed. "I'm in."

Asha stared at her for a long second. She leaned forward. "You know his study? The private one? That's my territory. He thinks the other girls are too clumsy for his 'important work,' so I'm the only one he lets clean in there." She rolled her eyes, a smirk tugging at her mouth. "The man's a fool. Practically leaves his secrets out for me to dust." She leaned in closer, her voice dropping even lower. "He has two different sets of books, Lyrra. *Two!*"

Asha's eyes were sharp and deadly serious. "My cousin Azru works the docks. And the serving girl at the tavern where the guards gamble? She's one of us. They drink and talk and drink some more, forgetting she's even there. But she doesn't forget anything... especially their secrets. And the women in the market? Like I said, we look out for each other—we've all served in the great houses for a long time. We know where the real secrets are kept." The barest hint of a smile. "They *are* this city. You want to ruin a man like Gisco? You don't use a sword. You use secrets." Her smile bloomed—dangerous and full of teeth. "And this city is full of them."

Lyrra reached under the table and brought out the dagger, laying it on the wood between them. The blade lay between them. *A promise.* "This is my vow," she said, her voice low and steady. "To you. We do this together, or not at all. *Your* freedom as much as mine."

Asha looked from the dagger to Lyrra's face. She placed her hand on the table, fingers inches from the blade. "Alright, my lady," Asha said, her voice quiet and pointed now. "You're the general. Give me my orders."

Lyrra's lips curved into the barest hint of a smile. "First," she said, "we stop the bleeding. We need to delay Gisco's message to Utica. And we need to get a message of our own to Hanno."

CHAPTER 20
A Ladder or a Wick

The plan looked terrifyingly simple. Asha's cousin, a nervous dockworker named Azru, was tasked with misplacing the shipping manifest for the fast ship to Utica. He returned that evening, a sheen of sweat on his upper lip.

"I can't," he stammered, twisting a piece of frayed rope in his hands. "The harbormaster, he watches that scroll like it might sprout wings and fly away. He's Gisco's man. They say he had the last man who 'lost' a manifest flogged in the public square. I can't, my lady."

Asha began to argue, but Lyrra held up a hand. She thought of the endless, infuriating Roman bureaucracy, a system built to be weaponized by those who understood its rules. "Don't misplace it," Lyrra said, her voice calm. "Question it. Is the weight of the amphorae recorded correctly? Is the tariff paid for *spiced* olive oil, or just oil? Create a clerical error. A dispute. Something that requires a magistrate's seal to resolve. Delay it with paperwork, not theft."

Azru stared at her, fear in his eyes. It was a language he knew. The next day, he reported that the ship to Utica was mired in a customs dispute that would take a week to unravel. They had bought time.

The second part of the plan was riskier. Lyrra, feigning a sudden craving for a specific type of honey-cake only sold in the lower city, sent Asha on an errand. Hidden in the basket, beneath a linen cloth, was a small, sealed clay tablet. The message was simple, written in a disguised hand: *The Peacock knows. Your debts are poison. Secure all assets.*

Asha passed the basket to another in her network, the baker's boy, who delivered it to Hanno's warehouse, a delivery of bread and figs no different from a dozen others.

For two days, Lyrra heard nothing. Nothing. She played the part of the dutiful fiancée—discussing floral arrangements with Sybil, enduring Gisco's proprietary touch on her arm. Meanwhile, the silence from the port was deafening. Every unexpected noise in the villa made her flinch, her heart seizing in her chest.

Every footstep in the hall was a guard coming to drag her away.

Then, on the third day, a gift arrived.

It was not from Gisco. A small, plainly dressed boy delivered a long, narrow box to the villa's kitchens, claiming it was a wedding gift for the handmaiden Asha, from her family. Asha brought it to Lyrra's chambers, her hands trembling as she set it on the table.

Inside, a rope lay coiled on a bed of dark wool. Simple sailor's rope, the kind used for mooring a ship. A small roll of papyrus tied to one end.

Her fingers wouldn't stop shaking. The papyrus crackled as she unrolled it. She tried to steady her hands. A short note. Bold handwriting—*familiar*. She knew that hand anywhere.

A rope can be a leash. Or it can be a ladder. Or it can be a wick to set something ablaze.

The choice is yours.

If you choose the ladder, this rope will be hanging from the western wall of the port warehouse at midnight, two nights before the wedding. Climb it, and we sail for a new life, leaving all this behind.

If you choose fire, then this rope is your wick... burn it all to the ground. I am with you, no matter what.

I will be waiting for your response.

She repeated one line. *The choice is yours.* Gods, she could barely breathe.

She looked at the rope, then at her own reflection in the silver mirror. She saw the girl who wanted to run. Just climb that rope, sail away into sunrise. But there was another woman staring back—the one with the dagger, the one who'd promised Asha her freedom. The one who knew that running would leave Gisco's power intact, always there, always watching, always waiting.

She closed her eyes, clutching the note. He had given her a choice. Now, she had to be brave enough to make it.

CHAPTER 21
At The Tombs

Lyrra sat in the quiet of her chambers, the coiled sailor's rope on the table before her. A ladder. An escape.

An insult.

She was seething. A hot, frantic energy under her skin that made it impossible to be still. She paced the length of the room, bare feet slapping against the cool mosaic floor. The rope wasn't an offer of freedom. It was an offer of retreat. A way for the timid Roman girl to be rescued while Gisco sat on his throne, laughing, telling the world how she'd fled his generosity.

No.

He gave her a choice. She would show him the one she was making.

She snatched the rope from the table, shoved it deep into the bottom of her dowry chest, and slammed the heavy lid. The sound was a definitive crack, like a bone snapping.

She found Asha, her voice low and urgent. "A message for the baker's boy. Now."

The message was two words, scratched onto a shard of pottery with the point of her new dagger.

Tombs. Tonight.

o   o   o   o   o

The air in the necropolis was cold. It smelled of damp earth. He was there, a shadow leaning against a stone wall. He didn't move as she got closer, just watched her.

She didn't say anything. She walked right up to him, grabbed the front of his tunic, and kissed him. A hard, messy kiss.

She pulled back, breathing hard. She couldn't stand still. She started pacing, kicking at loose stones, her hands waving in the air.

"Your note," she said, her voice shaky but rising. "A ladder? You want me to climb down a ladder and run away while that... that prick sits on his throne and calls me a coward?"

Hanno's eyes darted around the dark tombs, a silent plea for her to lower her voice. She ignored him.

"And for what? He thinks he can just... erase you? With a word? He thinks this thing..." She grabbed the heavy gold torc at her throat. "...makes me his property? Ugh. Get this—Asha says he's such a fool he probably can't even find his own dick in the morning!"

A frantic, slightly hysterical laugh bubbled out of her. "And she's right! He is a prick. A total and complete prick." Lyrra turned, pivoting her foot in the dirt. "But he's not even the real problem. It's his mother! Sybil. She's the one in charge. The 'asshole doing asshole things,' as Asha puts it."

She stopped pacing, planting her feet and turning to face Hanno, her voice dropping to a low, intense hiss. "So we're not running. We're not escaping. We're going to burn it all down. His name, her money, all of it. This isn't about escape anymore, Hanno. It's about justice."

She took a final, deep breath, her chest heaving. "Asha is with me. Her people are with me. I need to know… are you with me? Not to rescue me. To fight with me."

He just leaned against the tomb, arms crossed, and watched her. His face was unreadable, his expression giving nothing away.

He waited a second after she finished.

"Well?" she asked, the silence stretching her nerves thin.

He chuckled, a low, rumbling sound. "I'm just wondering what I'm supposed to do now."

"What do you mean?"

"My plan," he said, pushing off the wall, "was to rescue a timid Roman girl. Who is this?" He gestured at her. "This general? This fire-starter, with a sailor's mouth? What happened to the girl from the terrace?" A grin spread across his face." Where'd she go? Bring her back."

A real laugh tore out of her. She shoved him in the chest. "She's gone. You'll have to make do."

His grin vanished. Replaced by something else. Something hot. He caught her by the waist, his hands strong, and she looked at him—really looked at him. The man who saw her. The man who trusted her. And a thought, a wicked, liberating thought, just took over. She pushed him back against the stone of the tomb. She sank to her knees.

Her voice came out a husky whisper she didn't recognize. "Give me the serpent."

Lightning. The whole world went white for a second. She saw his face—shock, then awe, then something else. Something like surrender. His hands hovered near her shoulders. He didn't know what to do.

Good.

She didn't wait. Her fingers found the knot on his trousers. Undid it. The rough linen fell away and she pushed it down his thighs, her palms flat against his skin. Hard muscle. Tense.

He was... there. Just as she remembered. Big. Intimidating. But the fear was gone. Burned out of her. Now there was just this... hunger. This need to know. She reached out, her fingers tracing the thick vein that ran the length of him. He sucked in a breath. A sharp hiss. That sound. It was like a key turning in a lock deep inside her.

She leaned in. Her tongue flicked out. Just a taste. Salt. Musk. Him.

A groan rumbled in his chest and his hands finally found a home, tangling deep in her hair. Not pulling. Just holding on. Like he was the one who needed an anchor now.

This was her choice. Her hands. Her mouth. She took him in slowly at first. Learning. The smooth, slick head. The hard ridge of it. The texture of his skin. She teased him, circled him with her tongue, felt him pulse against her lips. She loved it. Gods, she loved the way his hips gave a little jerk. The way his knuckles went white where he gripped her hair. He was losing control. And she was the one taking it.

She pulled back. Just an inch. Let the cool night air hit his wet skin. He groaned, a raw sound of protest, his eyes flying open. She smiled. A slow, wicked smile she didn't even know she owned. Then she took him again. Deep. All the way. Her throat accepted all of him, and she felt a tremor go through his whole body.

He cried out, a muffled sound against her mouth. No more games. This was it. She found a rhythm, her head moving, her hand wrapped around the base of his cock, stroking. She could feel the tension coiling in him, the muscles in his thighs bunching like stone. He was so close. She wanted to feel it. She wanted to taste his surrender. Her offering.

A drop of rain hit her cheek. Fat and cold. Then another.

The storm was coming. It pushed her harder. He was groaning her name now, a desperate, broken sound. Hips bucking. She felt it—that final, violent clench. The shudder that wracked his whole body as he flooded her throat. Hot. Thick.

She swallowed. Every drop.

She stayed there, just for a second. Her cheek against his thigh. His hand still tangled in her hair, his whole body shaking. The taste of him on her tongue. The smell of him all around her. It wasn't just pleasure. It was… release. Not just his. Hers. All the fear, all the shame, all the years of being a good Roman daughter, a piece of property—gone. Burned away by this. She had faced the serpent. And it was hers.

Thunder cracked, a physical jolt through the ground. He pulled her to her feet, his eyes dark with an urgency that had nothing to do with what they'd just done. Shelter. He was pulling her deeper into the tomb, into the dark. Into safety, away from the storm.

The smart thing… Fuck the smart thing.

A wild laugh tore out of her, a sound she'd never heard herself make before. She dug her heels in, pulling him the other way.

Outside.

His eyes widened in confusion, a silent "What are you doing?" just before she dragged him past the stone awning.

The first drops of rain were fat and sparse, hitting the dry dust around them with little puffs. One hit her forehead, cold and shocking. Another hit his cheek. He wiped it away, still looking at her like she was insane.

And then the sky just… broke.

This was no drizzle. It was a sudden, hissing sheet of water, a roar that drowned out everything else. The world vanished behind a curtain of grey. In two seconds, her tunic clung to her like a second skin, heavy and cold. The rain plastered her hair to her face, streamed into her eyes, into her open mouth.

She threw her head back and just laughed. A stupid, open-mouthed laugh that was probably half rainwater. This was it. This was the opposite of the villa. The opposite of the still, perfect, suffocating air of her father's house. This was chaos. And it was glorious.

Hanno was just staring at her, rain dripping from his chin, a look of utter disbelief on his face. He saw her, really saw her—not a proper Roman lady, not an oligarch's prize, but this half-drowned, laughing creature. And then he was laughing too. A deep, booming laugh that she could feel in her chest even over the sound of the storm.

He lunged for her, and this time it wasn't a tease. He scooped her up, her feet leaving the muddy ground, and spun her around. She shrieked, her arms thrown around his neck, her face buried in the wet curve of his shoulder. He smelled of rain and earth and him.

He set her down, but he didn't let go. His hands framed her face, his thumbs wiping the water from her cheeks, a gesture of impossible tenderness in the middle of the deluge.

"You're crazy," he shouted over the roar of the rain.

"I know!" she shouted back, grinning.

And the grin was all it took. The playfulness vanished, replaced by a need so sharp it was a physical pain. The kiss wasn't a choice, it was a collision. It was messy, all teeth and open mouths, tasting of rain and him and the metallic tang of pure adrenaline. They couldn't get enough, couldn't get closer. Her hands were in his hair, pulling his face to hers. His hands were everywhere—on her back, her waist, her ass, pulling her tight against him.

The energy had to go somewhere. It was too much for a kiss. He broke away, his chest heaving, his eyes black holes in the grey light. He lifted her without a word, her legs wrapping around his waist instinctively. She felt the rough, cold stone of the tomb wall against her back, a solid anchor in the swirling chaos. He tried to push inside her, a desperate, fumbling attempt.

Gods, the fabric.

Her wet tunic was bunched up, a thick, stubborn barrier between them. His was the same. It wasn't working. It wasn't enough.

A frustrated groan escaped him. He let her down for a second, just long enough for his hands to grab the hem of her tunic and shove it upward, a rough, impatient gesture that bunched the cold, wet linen under her breasts. Her skin, exposed to the rain, prickled with goosebumps. He did the same to his own, hiking it up around his waist. Then he lifted her again, slamming her back against the wall.

This time, there was nothing between them but rain and heat.

He drove into her with a single, sharp thrust that made her cry out, a sound that was half pain, half pure, unadulterated pleasure. He filled her completely. The cold stone at her back, the cold rain on her face, and the burning, impossible heat of him inside her.

But the angle was wrong. He was straining to hold her up, his boots slipping in the mud. She could feel the tremor in his arms.

"No," she gasped against his mouth, "here."

She slid her legs from around his waist, her feet finding the slick ground. She grabbed his hand and pulled him, stumbling, a few feet away to a low, flat-topped sarcophagus. Its stone surface was slick with rain. She hitched herself up onto it, lying back on the cold, wet stone, her legs falling open in a clear, shameless invitation.

He came over her, his hands planting on either side of her head, caging her in. The rain fell on his back, running in rivulets down his arms. He looked down at her, his face a mask of raw, focused need. He entered her again, slower this time, a deep, deliberate slide that made her back arch off the stone.

And then they moved.

It wasn't a rhythm. It was a writhe. A desperate, rocking friction of wet skin against wet skin. The sound was obscene—the slap of their bodies, her gasps, his groans, all of it mingling with the steady drumming of the rain on the stone around them. Her hands scraped over his back, her nails leaving marks she couldn't see. She didn't care. She wanted to mark him. She wanted to claim this, to claim him. He met every frantic thrust, his hips slamming against hers, their bodies moving together in a fight for something more than release.

The pleasure was building again, a searing heat at her core, winding tighter and tighter. Her mind went blank. There was no Rome, no Gisco, no plan. There was only the rain, the cold stone under her, and the hot, unrelenting pressure of him, driving her toward the edge.

She cried out his name—not a whisper, a scream torn from her throat, a sound of pure, shattering release that was swallowed by a deafening crack of thunder.

She felt him follow a moment later, a deep, shuddering groan rumbling from his chest as he poured himself into her.

The storm passed as quickly as it had arrived. Leaving them shivering, slick with rain and sweat, clinging to each other in the sudden, dripping quiet...

He collapsed on top of her, a dead weight. His face was buried in her neck, his breathing loud and ragged in her ear. For a second, there was nothing. No storm, no Gisco, no plan. Just the feeling of his heart hammering against hers, the slick slide of their skin, and the steady, dripping sound of rain running off the stone tomb. The world had gone quiet.

Then the cold hit her.

Not the thrilling, shocking cold of the downpour. A different kind. A deep, seeping cold from the stone beneath her back, working its way into her bones. She was shivering. Violently. Her teeth started to chatter.

He stirred, lifting his head. He pulled out of her with a wet, final sound that echoed in the sudden silence. The connection was broken. She felt... empty. Untethered.

He helped her sit up. Her legs were shaking so badly she almost slid off the sarcophagus. She fumbled with her tunic, pulling the cold, sodden linen down over her thighs. It clung to her, useless. He did the same, his movements clumsy.

And then she looked at him. Really looked at him.

His hair was plastered to his forehead. A trickle of rainwater mixed with sweat ran from his temple. His chest was still heaving. He wasn't the Serpent from the sailors' stories. He wasn't a god in a storm. He was just a man. Shivering. Exhausted.

A man she had just tied to her insane, suicidal plan.

The reality of it hit her. *The wedding. The crowd. Gisco.* The dawning horror of what *she* was about to do. What she had asked *him* to do.

What have I done?

He must have seen it on her face. The shift. The terror. His expression hardened, the lover vanishing, replaced by the general. Her partner in treason.

He let her slide down until her feet touched the muddy ground. Her legs barely held her. There were no more words. Not for this. He kissed her one last time, a hard, final press of lips. It wasn't about passion. It tasted of rain and resolve.

"Go," he said, his voice rough. "Be safe."

She just nodded, unable to speak. She turned and melted back into the stormy darkness, not looking back.

She knew where she would see him next.

CHAPTER 22
Choosing the Fire

Lyrra sat in the quiet of her chambers, the coiled sailor's rope on the table before her. She closed her eyes and there it was. The ladder. Frantic climb in the dark, Hanno's hand pulling her onto the ship deck. Salt and freedom on the wind as they sailed toward a new sunrise, leaving Carthage and its cages behind.

Then she opened her eyes. The dagger lay hidden beneath a fold of silk. She saw a different vision now. Fire. The stunned faces of the city's elite. The shattering of a man's power. The risk was immense, the outcome uncertain. But it was a vision of justice. For herself. For Hanno. For Asha.

Her hands moved without hesitation. She picked up the rope, coiled it tight, and buried it in the bottom of her dowry chest, beneath those Roman linens she would never use.

When Asha entered the room, Lyrra was standing by the crimson silk of her wedding dress, which was laid out on the bed. Lyrra didn't speak. She simply lifted a fold of the heavy fabric, revealing the hilt of the dagger she had stitched within its seams.

Asha's breath quivered, her eyes wide. "Gods, Lyrra. You're really going to do it." The words were barely a whisper.

"He left me no other choice," Lyrra said, her own voice calm and steady. "He wants to erase a man's life for pride. He will not have it."

Asha nodded, her fear hardening into resolve. "The women in the market are ready. My cousin Azru will have the dockworkers spread the rumors at dawn. By the time you walk to the dais, half the city will know about Gisco's 'shipping losses'."

"Good," Lyrra said. She walked to the small brazier used for heating scented oils. She took a single, perfect saffron flower—the last remnant of Hanno's first secret message—and held it to the flame. It blackened and curled into ash. She wrapped the fragile, burnt offering in a scrap of linen.

"Give this to the baker's boy," she said, handing the small packet to Asha. "The message is one word."

Asha took it, her hand steady now. "Fire."

Lyrra nodded. "Fire."

The eve of the wedding was a blur of ritual and preparation—of scented oils and braided hair, of the rustle of silk and the quiet, steady hands of her co-conspirator. Finally, there was only the veil, gossamer-thin and embroidered with hundreds of tiny seed pearls.

As Asha lowered it over her face, the world dissolved into a pale, blurry haze. But behind the veil, Lyrra's vision had never been clearer. No more fear. Just purpose, cold and hard as the steel against her thigh.

CHAPTER 23
The Unveiling

The day of the wedding dawned unnaturally bright. Lyrra didn't move while two servants she didn't know draped her in a fortune's worth of crimson silk, the traditional color for a Carthaginian bride. The dress was heavy, intricate, and felt like armor.

Asha was not there. She was a whisper moving through the city, her network spreading like roots underground. The silence from her was Lyrra's only comfort. *It means the plan is in motion,* Lyrra reassured herself.

Sybil entered the room, her expression one of supreme satisfaction. She looked Lyrra over, not as a future daughter, but as a masterpiece she had acquired. "Perfect," she declared. "The picture of bridal modesty. You will do our family proud."

As Lyrra walked through the villa toward the great hall, she could hear the noise of the crowd. But beneath it, she could almost feel the whispers Asha had seeded, a current of rumor and doubt running beneath the polished marble floors. She focused on the weight of the dagger strapped to her inner thigh, a cold, secret promise against her skin.

The great hall was packed. Every powerful family in Carthage was present. At the far end of the hall, on a raised dais, Gisco waited. He was all masculine power, dressed in a tunic of the purest white, a golden laurel wreath on his dark hair. He looked every bit the king of his gilded world.

His smile was one of triumph as she approached. He had won. The rebellious Roman girl was tamed, veiled, and walking to him to be claimed.

Lyrra reached the dais and stood before him. The High Priest of Melqart began the long, droning invocation, his words flowing past her. She felt nothing. Her heart was cold, steady. Not a bride. A soldier.

The priest finished and turned to Gisco. "Do you take this woman, Lyrra of the house of Aemilius, to be your wife, to join your houses and your fortunes?"

"I do," Gisco said, his voice ringing with smug confidence.

The priest turned to her. "And do you, Lyrra of the house of Aemilius—"

He never finished the sentence.

Lyrra reached up with both hands and lifted her own veil. She cast it aside. It drifted to the marble floor, like a discarded shroud.

A collective gasp went through the hall. A bride did not unveil herself. She was unveiled by her husband, a symbolic act of possession.

Lyrra looked directly into Gisco's eyes. His smile faltered. Confusion settled on his face, then annoyance. She saw the exact moment he realized this was not part of the script.

She took a breath, her voice clear, steady, and carrying to every corner of the silent, stunned hall.

"No," she said. "I do not."

CHAPTER 24
The Shattering

The silence in the hall was absolute, a thick, heavy blanket of disbelief. A hundred of the city's most powerful oligarchs were frozen. Gisco's face was a mess of confusion, then fury, then the slow, hot creep of public humiliation.

"What is the meaning of this?" Sybil hissed from the side, her features hardening into a mask of cold fury. "Lyrra, you will not do—"

"I will," Lyrra said, her voice cutting through her future mother-in-law's. She kept her eyes locked on Gisco. "I will not be the wife of a man who conspires against Carthage."

A low, chaotic murmur rippled through the crowd. Some men exchanged dark, knowing looks. Others, like the corpulent senator Varro, merely looked annoyed by the interruption.

"You are hysterical," Gisco finally managed, his voice tight with rage. "You shame yourself."

"Shame?" Lyrra countered, taking a step forward. "Is it shameful to expose a man who secretly funnels grain from our city's emergency stores to sell to our rivals in Syracuse?"

The murmurs grew louder, more agitated. Varro shifted his weight, his eyes narrowing.

"Lies," Gisco spat. "The ravings of a madwoman!"

"He calls me mad," Lyrra said, turning to the crowd, her voice ringing with cold, clear logic. But just as their outrage began to coalesce, Varro stood up, his voice booming over the noise.

"A fascinating performance!" he declared. "The girl is clearly overwrought. Gisco, my friend, you should have chosen a bride with a stronger constitution." He turned to the crowd, his voice dripping with condescending reason. "Are we to trust the word of a spurned, hysterical woman over a man who has made us all rich?"

The momentum in the room faltered, then reversed. The murmurs shifted. Gisco's power was not so easily broken; it was built on the self-interest of every man in the room. He visibly straightened, his confidence returning.

"You see?" Gisco sneered, stepping toward her. "An entertaining fiction. But you have no proof."

"Is it, Varro?" Lyrra's voice cut through his, sharp and precise, turning on his staunchest defender. "Or is it that your own 'unfortunate' shipping losses last year were so conveniently covered by Gisco's generosity? Perhaps your ledgers are kept in the same scroll-case!"

Varro froze, his face turning a mottled purple. Gisco's sneer faltered.

"You want proof?" Lyrra's voice was still calm. She reached into a hidden fold of her crimson dress and produced a small, rolled piece of papyrus. "Asha has been a most diligent handmaiden." She unrolled the page and read a single, devastating line of accounting aloud. "*To Varro, for services rendered in the matter of the Sicilian grain fleet: ten talents of silver, recorded as cargo spoilage.*" She rolled the papyrus back up. "I have more."

On that cue, from the upper gallery, a half-dozen silent, stone-faced women—weavers, cooks, handmaidens—turned over their baskets.

Dozens of pages from the secret ledgers fluttered down onto the stunned crowd like poisoned snow.

The hall erupted. It was not a murmur now; it was a roar. Oligarchs scrambled, grabbing the pages from the air, from the floor. A cacophony of voices rose as they began to read the incriminating details aloud.

"—my contract with the Numidians!"

"—he sold the Tyre shipment to my cousin behind my back!"

"—Sybil's new jewels… billed to the city aqueduct project?!"

Paranoia tore through the room. Every man was now looking at his neighbor, his business partner, with raw, undisguised suspicion. The foundations of their world were shattering in real time.

Amidst the chaos, Lyrra's gaze found Sybil. The woman wasn't shouting. She wasn't moving. She was just… still. A point of absolute, chilling stillness in the center of the storm. She wasn't looking at her son. She was watching the chaos, her expression not one of a grieving mother, but of something else. Something cold. Calculating.

Then Sybil's eyes met hers.

She didn't scream. She didn't lunge. She slowly, deliberately, raised a single finger and pointed directly at Lyrra. Her finger sat there in the air as her eyes tightened with hate. Then, she drew that finger across her own throat. The gesture was silent. Chilling. Absolute. It was a promise.

Lyrra looked from Gisco's face, twisted with hate, to the chaos erupting around them. *This was her fire. She had struck the flint.* The shouts of ruined men filled the air. It should have sounded like chaos. To her, it sounded like a hymn.

But the hymn faded. The fire felt distant. All she could feel was the cold, silent promise of Sybil's gaze, a brand searing itself into her.

CHAPTER 25
The Victory Lap

The great hall exploded into chaos. Shouts, accusations, the crash of an overturned table laden with wine goblets. Gisco, his face raw with murderous hatred, lunged for Lyrra. Before he could take a step, his own guards grabbed him, their faces grim. Senator Varro was already barking orders at the guards, his voice cutting through the din, securing his own position amidst the ruin of his former ally. Sybil, her face a mask of stone, was now in a hushed, urgent conversation with another senator, her eyes cold and calculating. She was already cutting her losses. *Gisco.*

Then a hand clamped on Lyrra's arm. Asha. "This way," she hissed, her face flushed, eyes bright with a terrifying fire. She pulled Lyrra toward a door hidden behind a tapestry. "The whole villa is a hornet's nest. We use the tunnels."

The darkness of the servants' corridors swallowed them. The roar of the great hall faded to a dull thrum. Lyrra's legs felt like water; she stumbled, catching herself on the rough stone wall. "I did it," she whispered into the musty cavernous air. "Gods, Asha, I *actually* did it."

Asha led her to a small, hidden cellar and lit a single oil lamp. "Here," she said, pressing a heavy pouch of coins into Lyrra's hand. "Your share from the silk..." She paused, giving Lyrra a significant look. "...and a little extra from some... interested investors who believe in our new enterprise." She grinned, a flash of white in the gloom. "And this." She began unlacing the heavy crimson wedding dress. Asha helped her into a simple, practical tunic and trousers. The rough wool was the most comforting thing she'd ever felt.

They looked at each other. *Equals.* They did this together.

Lyrra reached out and gripped Asha's shoulder. "I can't go back to Rome," she said, the words a quiet admission of the cost. "And I'm leaving you here."

"You freed me as much as I freed you," Asha's voice was rough with emotion. She cleared her throat, her sharp wit returning. "Besides, someone has to stay and make sure they salt the earth where his reputation used to be." She pulled Lyrra into a fierce hug. "Now go. He's waiting. Live a life big enough for the both of us."

Lyrra ran, not looking back. The sewers were rank, a visceral transition from the perfumed prison she had left behind. The sewer stench was the smell of freedom. She emerged, blinking, into the chaos of the port at night. Just another face in the dark. She found the western warehouse and saw him—a silhouette against the moonlit wall.

He saw her and pushed off the wall to meet her. He didn't smile, not at first. He just looked at her, his gaze sweeping over her, her unbound hair, then locked on her gaze. The look in his eyes wasn't the hungry desire she knew. It was something deeper, quieter.

"The city is on fire," he said, his voice a low rumble of awe. "They're saying a Roman girl lit the match."

"Someone had to," she managed, her voice catching.

He pulled her in, his arms wrapping tight around her, his mouth finding hers. It wasn't a gentle kiss. It was hard, and desperate, and real. She clung to him, grounding herself in the solid warmth of his body, the taste of salt and night on his lips.

Everything else—the noise, the shouting, her entire life up to this point—just faded.

"My ship, she's ready," he murmured against her lips, his breath warm. "The *Desert Wind*. She's fast."

They walked hand-in-hand to the docks. Mago, who had once called her a 'stray,' now met her gaze and gave a single, sharp nod of respect. Bomilcar offered the barest hint of a smile. Lyrra straightened her shoulders, meeting their look without flinching.

As she stepped onto the gangplank, Lyrra took one last look back. She could just make out the lights of the villa on the Byrsa— a pinprick of fire in the hills. *Her prison.* Down below, the port churned with life. *Her escape.*

The ship pulled away from the dock, the shouts and smells of Carthage fading behind them. The sails caught the wind with a sharp crack, pulling them out into the dark, open sea. Lyrra stood at the railing, the sea spray cool on her face. She watched the lights of the city shrink until they were just embers, then sparks, and then they were gone.

CHAPTER 26
The New Map

The sun rose over an endless expanse of rolling water. The air, scrubbed clean of Carthage's smoke and fear, tasted of salt and nothing else. The sea wasn't the flat, menacing grey of Lyrra's voyage out; it was a brilliant, impossible blue, alive with light. The world had been washed clean, and there was only the sky, the sea, and the gentle creak of the ship's timbers.

She took a breath. A real one. *Freedom*, she thought.

Later, in the captain's cabin, Hanno unrolled a new map on the large wooden table. Crisp parchment, smelling of ink. "Where does your heart want to go, Lyrra?" He tapped a finger on the coastline of the Aegaeum. "Silk and Greek philosophy?" he said. Then his finger slid south. "Myrrh and the pharaohs?" He looked up at her, a grin playing on his lips. "Or we could just find a quiet vineyard in Hispania and get fat."

He leaned back. "So. Where to?"

She looked from the map to his face. Then she placed her hand flat in the center of the parchment, on no land in particular. On all of them.

He watched her hand, then looked back at her face. A slow grin spread across his lips. "Ah," he said, his voice full of quiet laughter. "An excellent choice."

A perfect, unspoken agreement. The grin on his face softened, as he took a step closer, his hand coming up to trace the line of her jaw. The planning was over. The celebration was about to begin. The tension broke as he let out a laugh. Then his expression shifted, the grin turning wicked. He lunged for her tickling her sides.

She shrieked with laughter, a sound so free and joyous it surprised them both, batting at his hands as he backed her against the wall. He captured her, spinning her around into a fierce, face-to-face embrace. Their laughter simmered down, and they just stared into each other's eyes, their chests heaving.

"You," he whispered, his voice thick with raw emotion and truth, "are trouble."

A breathless laugh escaped her. "You have no idea," she whispered, pulling his mouth to hers.

He scooped her up into his arms. A gasp of surprise escaped her, which immediately turned into a delighted, full-throated laugh. He didn't carry her to the bed. He needed her now. He lifted her onto the table. The map crackled beneath her—all those places they'd talked about, now just ink and parchment beneath her.

They couldn't get their clothes off fast enough. Her tunic caught on her elbow, then slid free. His trousers tangled around his ankles, kicked away. Laughing and fumbling. Desperate. Lyrra pulled her linen undergarment aside.

He wet his fingers, touching the head of his dick. He moved between her legs, and she guided him. When he entered her, it was with a single, perfect motion. A slow, deliberate joining. A sharp, shared gasp. Eyes locked. The initial, savage pace soon softened into something deeper. Steadier. The ship rocked beneath them. He moved slowly now, watching her face. Lyrra lay back against the map, her head resting on the coast of Iberia, her eyes half-closed, lost in the overwhelming sensation of him inside her, of the open sea around them, of a freedom so total it was dizzying.

"Hanno," she gasped, a laugh bubbling in her throat, a sound of pure, dizzying freedom. "I feel... I feel like I'm on top of the world."

He stilled inside her. She opened her eyes to find him looking at her, his expression frozen. Then his face began to twitch. A snort escaped him, then another. He tried to stifle it, but it was no use. A great, shuddering laugh burst out of him, a sound so powerful it broke their connection. He slipped out of her, stumbling back from the table, a hand clutching his stomach as he was overcome with a wheezing, tear-inducing fit of laughter. He collapsed against the far wall, sliding down to the floor.

"What?" Lyrra asked, sitting up, bewildered and slightly bereft. "What is it?"

He couldn't speak. He just pointed a trembling finger at her, then at the table, and managed to gasp out a single, choked word.

"Map..."

Her brow furrowed in confusion. She looked down at herself, at the crumpled, ink-drawn world beneath her bare skin. Her eyes widened. *On top of the world.*

A small giggle escaped her lips. Then another. And then she was gone, falling back onto the map in a fit of her own, a full-throated, belly-laugh of pure, absurd, unadulterated joy.

The last thing she saw before her vision blurred with happy tears was him, sitting on the floor, helpless with laughter, in the cabin of a ship sailing toward a future they would discover together, one ridiculous moment at a time.

ABOUT THE AUTHOR

Sylvie D. Harlowe writes spicy romances that explore the fiery intersection of society, psychology, and unapologetic desire. With a lifelong fascination for ancient and hidden worlds, a keen insight into the human heart, and a love for sprawling landscapes and placid bodies of water, she crafts tales of fierce heroines who defy convention and heroes who are both supportive and utterly devastating (in all the best ways). Sylvie's writing delves into themes of reclaiming agency, examining complex trauma, the universal power of passion, and the enduring quest for a "happily-ever-after", no matter the era or obstacle. When she's not unearthing ancient secrets or plotting her next adventure across varying times and locales, Sylvie might be found admiring ancient coins, spending time with her family, or simply enjoying the quiet beauty of nature.

CONNECT WITH SYLVIE
@sylvie.d.harlowe
on *TikTok*, *Instagram*,
and other platforms.